I DO, I DO...FOR NOW
JoAnn Ross

Harlequin Books

TORONTO • NEW YORK • LONDON
AMSTERDAM • PARIS • SYDNEY • HAMBURG
STOCKHOLM • ATHENS • TOKYO • MILAN
MADRID • WARSAW • BUDAPEST • AUCKLAND

ISBN 0-373-44001-4

I DO, I DO...FOR NOW

Copyright © 1996 by JoAnn Ross

"No one tickles your fancy more joyously than the incomparable JoAnn Ross."

—Melinda Helfer

JoAnn Ross, the author of over fifty novels, talks about writing one of the launch books for Love & Laughter: "Whenever I'm asked how much of my stories are based on real life, I usually answer that I make them all up. In this case, however, that's not entirely true. Many years ago the neighbor's nasty dog chased my kitten up a tree. Although everyone assured me Fang would come down when he was ready, I wasn't convinced. Hours later, when I couldn't resist his plaintive, terrified cries any longer, I decided to take matters into my own hands. But I needed bait to lure him down. My husband arrived home that evening just in time to see his very pregnant wife climbing down from the tree, the salmon I'd planned to bake for dinner tucked under one arm, a howling, squirming kitten under the other. So, when my fireman hero needed to rescue a kitten from a tree, I resurrected my plot. Fortunately, my return to earth was a great deal easier than Mitch's."

Don't miss these exciting, upcoming books from JoAnn Ross

From TEMPTATION, The Men of Whiskey River:
605—UNTAMED (October 1996)
609—WANTED! (November 1996)
613—AMBUSHED (December 1996)

From MIRA: SOUTHERN COMFORTS (September 1996).
And JoAnn's short story in NEW YEAR'S RESOLUTION: BABY, on sale at Christmas.

Don't miss any of our special offers. Write to us at the following address for information on our newest releases.

Harlequin Reader Service
U.S.: 3010 Walden Ave., P.O. Box 1325, Buffalo, NY 14269
Canadian: P.O. Box 609, Fort Erie, Ont. L2A 5X3

To Jay,
who can always make me laugh

1

MITCH CUDAHY was a genuine all-American hero. Although he'd be the first to tell folks that he'd only been doing his job, the twenty-seven-year-old Phoenix fire fighter had a medal from the mayor, a certificate of commendation from the fire chief, and most impressive of all, he'd even received a letter from the President, written on official White House stationery. It hung on the station wall, right beside the crayon drawings from Mrs. Bingham's first grade class, which were a thank-you to Ladder Company No. 13 for a tour of the firehouse.

In the weeks following his death-defying dash into a burning apartment building to rescue twin infant girls from the flames, Mitch had appeared on "Good Morning America," "The Today Show," "Nightline," "Ricki Lake," and had even been interviewed by Regis and Kathie Lee, making his very proud mother the star of her neighborhood.

So with all that going for him, what the hell was he doing up a tree, juggling an open can of tuna fish while trying to keep from falling on his butt?

"You're not high enough," the aggravated female voice complained from the ground. "You'll never reach Buffy from there."

"I'm doing my best, darlin'," Mitch said through clenched teeth.

He'd just reached for a neighboring limb when the one beneath his feet cracked. There was a chorus of gasps from the crowd gathered below him as he managed to grab onto a branch above his head. As he hung there, dangling high above the desert floor, Mitch didn't feel much like a hero. He was also extremely grateful that Kathie Lee wasn't here to see this.

"Now look what you did," the seven-year-old girl scolded. "You dropped the tuna fish."

Tempted to suggest the smart-mouthed little kid rescue her own damn cat, Mitch reminded himself that all-American heroes were not allowed to cuss at kids. But that didn't stop him from cursing beneath his breath—ripe, pungent expletives directed at Buffy the adventurous Siamese, the damn bureaucratic animal control guys who'd decided that rescuing treed cats wasn't in their job description and yes, even sexy, blond Meredith Roberts of KSAZ, for showing up with her TV cameraman to capture his indignity on videotape.

Yet even as irritated as he was at most of the western world at that moment, Mitch saved his harshest condemnation for himself.

Hero?

How about chump?

The muscles in his arms were about to give out and his hands were sweating. With a mighty effort, he managed to pull himself up on to the limb. Straddling it, he found himself staring straight into the oblique blue eyes of a seal point kitten.

"You realize, of course, that you've caused a lot of people a great deal of trouble," Mitch said to the terrified kitten. The cat's tail, fluffed up to three times its normal size, was twitching back and forth like a pendulum. "But it's okay now. We're going to get all four paws back on solid ground.''

When he reached for the kitten, it backed up, arched its back and began hissing like a burst radiator hose.

''Come on, cat.'' He was unable to keep the edge of frustration from his coaxing tone. ''Look, there's a little girl down there who's got a can of tuna fish with your name on it.''

Inching forward, Mitch forced down his irritation and began talking to the reluctant animal in the same rational, calm tone he'd used on more than one occasion to convince a frightened civilian to jump from a third-story window into the net below.

''And not just any ordinary old cat chow stuff,'' he crooned. ''This is genuine, water-packed white albacore we're talking about, Buffy. The caviar of canned tuna.''

The closer Mitch got, the louder the cat's howling became—a grating, particularly Siamese complaint that affected Mitch's already touchy nerve endings like fingernails scraping across a chalkboard.

''That's my girl.'' The kitten was inches away. Pasting a huge, false smile on his face, Mitch made a grab for it.

Unfortunately, the cat was quicker. It leapt deftly out of his grasp and as he struggled to regain his balance, it landed, razor-sharp claws extended, smack in the middle of his back.

''Dammit!''

It was a roar, a bellow of fury mixed with pain that only made the howling kitten dig in deeper. Tempted to peel the cat off and fling it into the neighboring county, Mitch remembered—just in time—the television crew filming from the ground.

''You're just damn lucky we've got witnesses, you miserable, mangy fur bag.'' Grinding his teeth against the needle-sharp pain, he gingerly made his way back down the tree, the kitten's strident complaints ringing in his ear.

About ten feet from the ground, the cat bailed out, abandoning the relative safety of Mitch's back like a teenage dragster peeling away from a red light.

Buffy the Flying Kitten took a patch of Mitch's skin with her, and his bellowed curse made that scene unsuitable for the TV station's family audience. Unfortunately, the shot of all-American hero Mitch Cudahy's three-point landing in a spreading cholla did made the evening news.

Mitch's mother, always eager to see her famous son on television, was thrilled.

WHILE MITCH was playing the reluctant hero, Sasha Mikhailova, recent émigré to the United States, sat in a government office across the city, scared to death. She was also determined not to show it. Especially to the man who'd been a constant source of aggravation for the past month. Just as Superman had Lex Luther and Batman had The Riddler, Sasha had been cursed with Mr. Donald O.—for obnoxious, she thought—Potter.

Deported.

"You can't possibly be serious," she said, but she knew he was. The word tolled in her mind like a death knell. Her lips began to tremble; she managed, just barely, to control them as she looked around the cramped office that offered not a single clue to the man seated across the government-issue black metal desk. There were no family photos, no newspaper cartoons taped to the side of the desktop computer, no personal mementoes of any kind.

"The government doesn't make jokes, Ms. Mikhailova," he said, his voice as stiff as his manner.

As she looked across the unrelentingly neat desktop at her nemesis, she couldn't help thinking what her employer—and friend—had recently called him when he'd first shown up at the diner during the lunch rush hour. *Squinty-eyed weasel.*

The term, she decided, definitely fit. In all her twenty-four years, she'd never met a more mean-spirited individual. And considering all the bureaucrats she'd had to deal with to get to this country in the first place, that was really saying something.

"A lack of humor seems to be a universal trait where governments are concerned." Although her nerves were humming, Sasha lifted her chin fearlessly. "However, your government has made a mistake." She decided, for discretion's sake, not to mention that the mistake was mostly his. "You cannot deport me."

He arched a pale blond brow, licked the tip of his index finger and began flipping through the thick pages of her immigration file.

"It states here that when you first requested a visitor's visa, you declared yourself to be a nurse—"

"I worked as a surgical nurse. In St. Petersburg." She'd planned to attend nursing school here in the United States, to earn her license to practice, as soon as she'd settled down. Unfortunately that plan, like so many others, had turned out to be impossible, given the fact that she'd moved around like a Ukrainian gypsy since her arrival in New York one year ago.

"And then you were an English teacher?" His voice was thick with disbelief.

"Only part-time."

They'd gone over the same things the half-dozen other times she'd been summoned downtown to his office. He had all the information in her file. So why was he torturing her this way? Sasha decided he enjoyed toying with her emotions the same way a fat cat enjoyed tormenting a cornered mouse.

"My mother was a translator for the U.S. consulate in Leningrad. She taught me English from the time I was a very young child, so I was able earn the additional money necessary to come to this country by tutoring students after my shift at the hospital."

She was not surprised when he ignored her explanation as he had so many times before. "And now you're a waitress."

The amount of scorn he heaped on her current occupation made her temper flare. Counting to ten, first in her native Russian, then in her adopted English, she overcame her irritation and met his derisive gaze with a defiant look.

"Waitressing is good, honest work."

"Point taken," he said, surprising her by agreeing with her. Too late, Sasha realized she'd been set up. "That being the case, you certainly shouldn't have any trouble finding a job waiting tables back home."

His thin lips curved into a sneer. "Especially now that McDonald's has opened up shop in Russia."

Sasha tossed her dark head, sending the lush waves bouncing. She refused to let him bait her. Not when so much was at stake. "You cannot deport me."

The nasty smile reached his eyes, confirming her suspicions that he was thoroughly enjoying himself at her expense. "Want to bet?"

She'd studied the immigration laws carefully before coming to this country. When she'd arrived in New York, she'd gone to an attorney who'd taken her money and assured her that she was on firm legal ground. Two days later, he'd moved out of the storefront office and left no forwarding address.

He'd been only the first in a very long line to steal her nest egg. But that was no longer a problem because she'd spent the last of her hard-earned funds on the Greyhound bus ticket that had brought her from Springfield, Missouri, here to Phoenix.

"My father..." Embarrassed when her voice cracked, she felt the hot sting of furious, frustrated tears at the backs of her eyelids.

No. She would not cry! Sasha Mikhailova had the blood of czars running through her veins, along with that of a U.S. Confederate major, who'd reportedly done the O'Brien family proud fighting alongside Stonewall Jackson at the first Battle of Manassas.

Her Russian ancestors were hot-tempered, emotional aristocrats; her Irish ancestors were hot-tempered Celtic rebels who'd escaped County Cork one step ahead of the British sheriff. She would not give this sadistic little bureaucrat—this squinty-eyed weasel!—the satisfaction of making her weep in public.

She hitched in a deep breath and prayed for calm as she resolved not to crumble. "My father is an American."

He eyed her uncompassionately over the metal frame of his reading glasses. "Do you have any idea, Ms. Mikhailova, how many people, on any given day, tell me that same thing?"

"In my case, Mr. Potter, it is true."

"That's what they all say." He briskly stamped the manila file that represented a world of hope. A lifetime of dreams. "You have until Wednesday at 10:00 a.m. to compile the documents necessary to prove your case. If you can't, a deportation hearing will be scheduled for the following day. And then, Ms. Mikhailova, you will be put on the next plane back to Russia."

After making a notation on his desk calendar, he closed the file and placed it in a metal basket on the filing cabinet behind his desk.

Case closed.

Her life ruined.

Just like that.

"You would schedule this hearing so soon?"

He sighed, took off the glasses and gave her a stern look. "We've been through this before. You were granted a temporary visa in order to locate your alleged father—"

"He is not alleged!" Her flare of temper, which she could no longer restrain, brought much needed color into her pale cheeks.

She tilted her chin in a way that dared him to argue this all-important point. "All my life, while I was growing up, my mother told me stories about my father." Exciting, wonderful stories that had made the dashing American reporter who'd swept her mother off her feet and kept her warm during that frigid Leningrad winter seem larger than life.

"That's undoubtedly all they were," he sniffed. "Stories."

It was not the first time the horrid immigration officer had suggested such a possibility. The other times, in an attempt to prevent annoying him—and getting into more trouble—Sasha had dared not challenge his remarks. This time she decided she had nothing to lose.

"My mother, Mr. Potter, was not a liar." Maya Mikhailova had been the most honest, kindest woman Sasha had ever known. Since her mother's death eighteen months ago, there had not been a day that Sasha hadn't missed her wise advice, her warmth, her love.

"We're getting off the point." Frustration edged his voice and he waved his hand, brushing off her argument as he might a pesky insect. "The point I am attempting to make, Ms. Mikhailova, is that during your past year in this country, you have not resided at the same location—or for that matter, in the same city—for more than ninety days at a time—''

"It was important to keep searching."

He frowned at the interruption. "Perhaps it was important to hide your tracks." The accusation was, of course, preposterous. It was also one she'd heard from him before.

"I wanted to hide nothing."

"That's what you say. But I believe differently." He gave her a smug look over the tent of his fingers. "And unfortunately for you, the U.S. government tends to take the word of a sworn immigration officer over an alien who is attempting to circumvent the laws of this land by disappearing into the general—legal—population."

His evil, superior smirk made Sasha squeeze her damp hands tightly together in her lap to keep from giving in to the very strong temptation to slap the smile off his face. She had no doubt that he'd have not a single qualm about calling the police, which would, of course, result in her immediate deportation. Which would undoubtedly give Mr. Donald O. Potter vast pleasure.

He stood behind the desk, signaling that the interview was over. Sasha couldn't help wondering if his less-than-average stature explained his seeming need to push people around so cruelly.

"Ten o'clock next Wednesday," he reminded her. "You are, of course, entitled to legal counsel."

This was Friday, which gave her only four more days. Sasha's mind whirled. How was she going to find her father in so short a time when she hadn't been able to locate him in the past twelve months? And where was she to find the money for yet another lawyer?

She felt as if an iron fist was clutching at her heart as she left the cold, sterile government office. Determined not to reveal her pain to all the clerks who were buzzing around like busy worker bees, Sasha held her sable head regally high. Her back was straight as an arrow and as she marched past the other grim-faced resident aliens waiting to learn their individual fates, she was reminded of her long ago royal Russian ancestors.

Granted, this was not a fatal verdict. Still, as Sasha waited for the elevator to arrive, she thought she knew something of what her mother's relatives had felt as they'd prepared to face the Red Army's firing squads. As the metal elevator doors closed behind her, she found herself alone with a dark-suited man who reeked of some no doubt expensive but suffocating cologne. And adding to her discomfort, instead of watching the lighted numbers above the door as everyone else did while riding in an elevator, he couldn't seem to stop looking at her breasts.

Sasha had known it was a mistake to wear the snug uniform, especially when she would have preferred her single good black suit. But she knew from experience that she'd be kept waiting hours past her appointment time, which would not give her time to stop by the rooming house to change her clothes before work.

She kept her eyes straight ahead as she exited the elevator ahead of the other passenger, but she felt his predatory gaze all the way out of the building. Then she stood outside the towering black-glass office building, frustration escalating to the boiling point as she watched the city bus pull away from the curb. It would be at least ten minutes before another one arrived.

Which would, unfortunately, make her late to work.

Which meant she'd miss Mitch Cudahy when he picked up dinner for the firemen of Ladder Company No. 13. Although Sasha knew that the chances of an American hero looking twice at a mere waitress, let alone one who was shorter, darker, and far less stylish than the willowy blondes she knew he favored, ever since Mitch had arrived, sirens wailing, to put out a fire she'd accidentally started in the diner's kitchen, her heart had steadfastly refused to listen to her head.

After dousing the flames, he'd amazed her by apologizing for the three inches of water on the green-and-white checkered linoleum floor. Sasha had gazed into the depths of his eyes—their crystal blue absolutely riveting in his handsome, soot-smudged face—and against every bit of pragmatism she possessed, had fallen hopelessly, head over heels in love.

After that fateful day, whenever he came into the diner, with his cocky masculine stride, his compact body looking so wonderfully fit in the navy blue T-shirt and jeans favored by the city firemen, Sasha would feel light-headed and giddy.

The thought of having to leave Phoenix, to leave America, to never see Mitch again, was one more depressing thing in an already ghastly day.

She sighed, looking up at the clear blue sky. The morning rain had stopped. That, at least, was something.

She waited at the bus stop, her mind whirling, tossing up problems without solutions, dilemmas without answers. For a fleeting moment she considered running away, like the dreadful immigration officer had suggested she might be planning to do.

But where would she go? And how long could she hide before the government discovered her and sent her back to St. Petersburg in disgrace?

Her thoughts on the logistics of pulling off such an admittedly risky—not to mention highly illegal—plan, Sasha didn't see the pizza delivery truck speeding down the street until it shot through a puddle in front of her, splashing a wave of muddy water that drenched the front of her bubblegum-pink uniform.

2

IT WAS MORE than forty-five minutes before the bus finally showed up.

"It took you long enough to get here," the elderly woman in front of Sasha complained.

"Hey, don't blame me." The driver, who looked more like a roadie for a heavy metal band than a city employee, shrugged uncaringly. "The scheduled bus broke down."

"What about the one after that?"

"Do I look like Dan freaking Rather?" he retorted as he punched her card. "How should I know?"

"Young man, I have been riding this route every day for twenty-five years." The woman snatched her card back and jammed it into her already overstuffed shopping bag. "And never, in all that time, have I experienced such rudeness. I've a good mind to report you to your supervisor."

"You've got me trembling in my boots," he snarled in return.

As the woman stomped down the aisle, the driver leered at Sasha. "Well, hello." His eyes, hidden behind a pair of purple sunglasses, slid over her, taking in the muddied uniform. "Looks like you've had a rough day, sugar."

Although she certainly did not approve of the way he'd spoken to the previous passenger, Sasha was in no mood to enter into a confrontation with yet another government employee.

"I have had better." She held out her card.

"Well," he said, "this is my last run for the day. You need any help getting out of that wet outfit, just let me know."

The lewd suggestion was every bit as annoying as the immigration officer's earlier derision. "I do not think that will be necessary."

"If you're through insulting old ladies and trying to pick up waitresses, do you think we could get this show on the road?" an irritated blue-suited Yuppie type behind Sasha inquired.

"Hold your water, man." The driver punched Sasha's card, purposefully brushing his fingers over hers as she took it back.

Assuring herself that this had to be the low spot of her day, that things could not possibly get any worse, Sasha sank onto a hard seat midway down the aisle.

Although she hated the idea of being late for work, Sasha couldn't help feeling somewhat grateful for the delay. Because, as much as she looked forward to seeing Mitch Cudahy, she couldn't bear the idea of his seeing her looking so disheveled. Once again, she compared herself with his latest lover, a sleek, blond television news reporter, and once again Sasha realized that her fantasies of a life with the sexy fireman were exactly that—fantasies.

In front of her, two teenagers sat, heads together as they exchanged warm looks and soft murmurs and light kisses. Their hands were never still, stroking each other's hair, arms, faces all the way up Central Avenue.

Although no one could pay her to relive her own tumultuous teenage years, Sasha couldn't help being just a little envious. And when the boy bent his head and gave the girl a hot, lingering kiss that was obviously a prelude to many more before the night was over, she felt the ache all the way to her toes.

She'd never, in all her twenty-four years, had any man look at her that way. She'd never had any man kiss her that way. And until Mitch, she'd never met a man she'd even wanted to kiss her with such passion.

She closed her eyes and rubbed her temples where the Potter-caused headache throbbed painfully. With a six-hour shift yet to get through, Sasha could only hope that tonight would be a light one.

As the bus pulled up to the curbside stop on busy Camelback Road, Sasha viewed the shiny red fire truck parked outside the diner and groaned. Apparently she wasn't the only one who was late today.

She debated staying on the bus, riding to the next stop, then walking back. But she was already late for work; it would be wrong to leave Glory Seeger to pick up the slack simply because she was uncomfortable having the man of her dreams witness her looking like some homeless person.

"He never notices you anyway," she told herself as she exited the bus with the teenagers who were so besotted with each other. Reminding herself that she had far more problems to worry about than the lack of a lover, Sasha squared her shoulders, took a deep breath, pushed open the diner door and immediately found herself face-to-face with Mitch, who was on his way out.

CONTRARY to what she believed, Mitch had definitely noticed Sasha. He'd noticed her thick, wavy sable hair, her flashing dark eyes that revealed every emotion and the full rosy lips she was always forgetting to paint.

Since he was male, and human, he'd certainly noticed that her uniform fit a bit too snugly over her lush curves and that although she wasn't tall, her legs were long and firm, with an attractive fullness at the back of her calves.

He'd also noticed, over the aroma of hickory smoke from Glory's famed barbecued ribs, that the painfully shy waitress smelled damn good.

There had been a time, during a two-day lull between women, that he'd considered asking her out. But then Meredith Roberts had shown up at the fire station to interview him and one thing had led to another, and by the time the cameraman had packed up his videocam and equipment, Mitch had accepted her offer to take in the Cardinals football game from the television station's executive box.

They'd been dating for about three weeks now. And although he thoroughly enjoyed his single life and had no intention of ever settling down with any one woman for any extended length of time, he did tend toward serial monogamy. Which meant that he'd never gotten around to asking Sasha out as intended. But he'd continued to look.

Today, however, the sight was anything but appealing. She looked as if she'd gone through a car wash. Without the car.

"What the hell happened to you?"

It was then that Sasha burst into tears.

Terrific. This was all he needed, Mitch thought as the question he'd unthinkingly blurted sent Sasha into a torment of noisy weeping that had the fireman behind him looking at him as if he were an ax murderer.

This was just one more lousy thing in an already rotten day. After falling out of the tree, he'd spent an hour having cactus needles picked out of his flesh. He figured that he had more holes in him than a damn sieve and had arrived at the diner in a filthy mood.

"What the hell did you say to the poor girl, Cudahy?" Jake Brown growled. Jake was his brother-in-law and also his best friend. But the look he was giving Mitch right now was anything but friendly.

"I only asked what happened to her," Mitch retorted, his mood worsening by the moment.

"Mitchel Cudahy!" The booming voice coming from behind the chipped Formica-topped counter reminded him of his uncle Dan Cudahy, who worked as a logger in southern Oregon. With her wide shoulders and arms the circumference of Virginia hams, Glory Seeger even looked a bit like his uncle Dan. But without the mustache. "What are you doing, making my best waitress cry?"

"I didn't do anything!" Mitch turned to Sasha for confirmation.

Lord, the lady was really pitiful. Unlike the women he was used to, who could weep genteelly on occasion to gain their own way, Sasha was bawling like a baby. Her dark gypsy hair was a wild tangle over shoulders that were shaking like the L.A. Coliseum during an earthquake. Tears were streaming down her face like the Niagara over the falls, and her nose was as red as Rudolph's. There was an enormous wet brown stain covering the front of her Pepto-Bismol-pink skirt.

Even as he told himself that he hadn't done anything to cause this outburst, that he owed the sweet-smelling, Russian-born waitress nothing but a tip whenever she served him a cup of coffee and a piece of Glory's incomparable pecan pie, Mitch felt the familiar, unbidden sense of responsibility raise its nagging head.

It was the damn cat all over again. Sasha was a grown woman. The fact that she'd managed to make it out of Russia and come to the U.S. in the first place proved that she was more than a little capable of taking care of herself. Besides, whatever her problem, it had nothing to do with him.

He'd done his good deed for the day.

So why couldn't he just leave well enough alone?

Mitch wanted desperately just to walk past her and get back to work. Instead he sighed, set the foam containers he was carrying on a wobbly white wooden table close by, then took hold of her quaking shoulders. "Hey, Sasha." His smile was friendly and encouraging, not unlike the one he'd first given that ungrateful kitten. "Whatever it is, darlin', it can't be all that bad."

Darlin'. It was a word Mitch used indiscriminately with women in general. Today he'd already tossed it at the cat's seven-year-old owner and Meredith—even though he'd been ticked off about her bringing along a cameraman to record his indignity. He'd also used it on the pretty blond nurse who'd wielded those treacherous tweezers at Good Samaritan Hospital, and who, after plucking the cactus needles from his bare ass had given him her telephone number.

It was an all-purpose, friendly endearment. It didn't mean anything. Not really.

But when Sasha heard that drawled "darlin'," that same tender term she'd dreamed about so many times over the past weeks, her yearning heart turned a series of dizzying somersaults. For a fleeting, wonderful moment, hope sang its clear sweet song through her veins.

Then she made the mistake of looking up into Mitchel's thickly lashed eyes. The pity she saw in those crystal blue depths stimulated a fresh torrent of hot tears.

"Christ." Mitch wondered what he'd done now. He turned to Glory, who was watching the little drama, meaty arms folded over her abundant chest, her expression every bit as daunting as the meat cleaver she was holding.

"Would you please do something?" Mitch demanded with overt frustration. He'd had his fill of other people's problems today.

"You're the one who made the poor little girl cry." Glory's broad face reminded him of a threatening dark thunderhead. "*You* do something."

Mitch turned to Sasha, who'd turned her back and had buried her face in her hands. Her life was none of his business, he reminded himself yet again. It had nothing to do with him.

Aw, hell. . . .

"You know, darlin'," he said soothingly, "if you don't turn off the waterworks, you're liable to flood this place worse than I did when I put out the grease fire in your kitchen."

At the reminder of that fateful day when she'd fallen so totally, helplessly, in love with this man who was now witnessing her humiliation, Sasha's response was to sob louder.

Mitch threw up his hands. "I give up." The lady was about as volatile as an open can of gasoline next to a lit match. Having already used up his daily store of patience even before he'd arrived at the diner, Mitch sought assistance from his brother-in-law.

"You're used to dealing with hysterical females. Talk to her." The way Mitch figured it, any man who could handle Katie Cudahy Brown's PMS-induced tantrums could undoubtedly calm this sobbing, near-hysterical woman down.

"Ain't that just like a man," Glory broke in before Jake could answer. "Breaking a woman's heart, then leaving someone else to clean up his mess."

"Mess?" Mitch couldn't believe this. "What mess? What are you talking about?"

"I'm talking about whatever you did to Sasha." If looks could kill, the diner owner's glower would have put Mitch six feet under. "So help me, God, Mitchel Cudahy, hotshot hero or not, if you dared to get this poor, sweet, innocent girl in the family way—"

"What?" Mitch immediately went beyond disbelief to horror. He might not be a monk, but he was definitely not the irresponsible bastard Glory had just accused him of being. Hell, he'd practiced safe sex before it had gotten popular. "I didn't... I never... Whatever gave you the idea—"

"Mitch?" Jake finally entered into the discussion. His expression, Mitch noted with consternation, was suddenly as serious as Glory's.

"Dammit!" He took hold of Sasha's shoulders again and spun her around. "Tell them," he demanded as she lowered her hands from her face and stared up at him through glistening dark eyes, "tell them we've barely said two words to each other the entire time you've worked here."

"That doesn't prove a thing," Glory insisted. "My first three husbands never said all that much, either. In bed or out. Which is one of the reasons I divorced them. But that didn't stop the jerks from leaving me with five babies to raise."

"Sasha." Although it took a herculean effort, Mitch managed to draw in a deep breath that allowed him to inject a note of almost reasonable calm into his tone. "We both know that whatever is bothering you has nothing to do with me."

He gave her an encouraging smile and ran his palm down her dark hair, then jerked his hand away when he saw Glory's eyes narrow even more and realized the caress, meant to soothe, might, under the circumstances, look like something far more intimate.

"So why don't you do me a great big favor and get me off the hook by telling Glory and Jake that I'm just an innocent bystander here."

That wasn't true. Not really. The fact of the matter was that Mitch was, if not the cause, at least the trigger for her tears. But seeing the naked distress written all over his handsome face, and honestly appalled at how Jake and Glory had misunderstood the situation, Sasha dragged in a deep, shuddering breath that had the unfortunate side effect of drawing Mitch's rebellious eyes to her breasts, a movement that did not go unnoticed by Jake, who continued to frown at his brother-in-law.

"M-Mitch is r-right." She forced the ragged words through trembling lips. "He did nothing." She felt the strong fingers on her shoulders relax ever so slightly.

"See?" He shot the skeptical pair an I-told-you-so look over his shoulder.

"I don't know," Glory mused grumpily. "Maybe she's just covering up for you."

When his fingers tightened again, digging painfully into her shoulders, Sasha shook her head. "No." She hitched in another deep breath that threatened to pop a button. "It's not Mitch's fault. And I apologize for upsetting everyone."

Sasha tried to force a wobbly smile and failed miserably. "It is nothing," she insisted. Her lips began to tremble again. "Really."

Although Mitch was ready to leave, relieved to escape the uncomfortable emotional female scene, Jake wasn't about to let the matter go so easily.

"Obviously it's something." He added the foam cartons he was still holding to the ones Mitch had left on the table and pulled out a chair covered in cracked red plastic. "So why don't you sit down and tell us all about it, honey?"

"You are very kind, Jake." Sasha rubbed at her shining, red-rimmed eyes with the backs of her hands, reminding Mitch of how that unhappy little cat owner had looked when he'd first arrived on the scene. "But it is not necessary." She looked past the two firemen to Glory. "I was late today. It is past time I began working."

"You see any customers around here?" Glory asked. Her eyes swept the small storefront diner, taking in the empty tables and the row of red booths along a wall decorated with brightly colored posters touting Louisiana hot sauce. "Sit down, girl. And spill the damn beans before they get you all choked up again. Besides," she added, when she got the impression Sasha was about to continue arguing, "a bawling waitress tends to spoil customers' appetites."

She turned to Mitch. "Get the poor girl a drink of water."

After the way Glory had attacked him without provocation, Mitch was tempted to suggest that, since she owned the place and he was merely a customer, it was her damn responsibility to get her crazy, overwrought waitress a drink.

However, ever since the fire, a grateful Glory had insisted on supplying the meals whenever it was his turn to cook for the crew of the fire station located down the street. Since Mitch's culinary repertoire consisted of hot dogs, hamburgers and a very pedestrian spaghetti utilizing canned sauce, both he and the rest of the fire fighters were more than a little grateful for the meat loaf, barbecue chicken and ribs Glory provided. That being the case, he held his tongue.

He crossed the room, went behind the counter and poured ice water from the pitcher into a green plastic glass. When he returned and held the glass out to Sasha, the blatant appreciation in her dark brown eyes reminded him uncomfortably of a cocker spaniel he'd had as a kid.

"Thank you, Mitch." When she felt her cheeks burn with embarrassment, she looked away and concentrated on the steady flow of traffic out the window.

Embarrassed at receiving such a degree of gratitude for such a simple gesture, Mitch merely shrugged in response.

But as he watched her lift the glass to her mouth, he found himself wondering, not for the first time since Glory had hired her, if those lush, rosy lips were as succulent as they looked.

All too aware of Mitch watching her as she took a sip of the icy water, Sasha dragged her attention back to her less-than-ideal situation.

Glory, Mitch and Jake knew that she was searching for her father, but she hated the thought of having to tell them more of her private family problems. Glory, however, had treated Sasha more like a daughter than an employee, and knowing that her employer would just keep after her until she revealed what had her so upset, Sasha slowly, painfully, related the details of her afternoon interview with the horrid Mr. Donald O. Potter.

"That damn weasel," Glory said, right on cue.

"That's not fair," Jake said. "Sending you back to Russia just because you haven't been able to find your father."

"Unfortunately, laws are not always fair," Sasha murmured.

It was a lesson she'd learned early in life. Which was another reason that the stories her mother had told her about life in America—where supposedly the people themselves made the laws—had seemed almost like fairy tales. She lifted the cool glass to her temple, where a headache was pounding with unrelenting force, and sighed.

"Well, it's obvious that we can't let them send you back," Jake declared.

He was such a nice man, Sasha considered. Always ready with a smile for her, always asking about her day, showing her new photos of his baby daughter. He routinely overtipped and whenever she'd complain that he'd left far too much beside the empty white coffee cup, he'd invariably wink and tell her to put the money into her search fund.

Still, as nice as Jake was, Sasha knew he did not possess the power to solve this dilemma.

"I don't think I have a choice."

"Hell, girl, everyone has a choice," Glory insisted. "That's what America is all about."

The loyalty of these people she'd known only a few weeks moved Sasha tremendously. As she thought about how much she would miss them, once she was deported, she felt a renewed threat of tears. Not wanting Mitch to think her a complete idiot, she managed to keep the floodgates closed this time.

She twisted her hands together in her lap. "I was thinking of running away," she admitted in a voice that was little more than a whisper. Still, hearing the words out loud made them suddenly seem almost possible.

Her mind began to whirl, considering the possibilities. She'd heard Seattle was nice. And, of course, there was Los Angeles. In a city so large it should not be difficult to disappear.

Perhaps Montana. She could get a job on a ranch, far away from civilization, cooking for cowboys. Upset as she was, Sasha conveniently overlooked the fact that she was a terrible cook.

"Running away is never the answer," Jake said, interrupting her agitated thoughts. He shook his head. "Especially in this case. You'd have broken the law and immigration would eventually catch up with you."

"Which would mean immediate deportation," Glory pointed out. "You can't give that squinty-eyed, chinless weasel the satisfaction of getting rid of you that easily."

Mitch, Sasha noticed, had not joined in the conversation. He was standing there, absently rubbing his jaw as he stared out the front window of the diner, his thoughts seemingly a million miles away.

"The law is the law." She repeated what Mr. Donald O. Potter had told her. "I have four days to find my father. If I cannot locate him in that time, I will be sent back to Russia."

"We could hire a private detective," Jake suggested. "Granted, four days isn't all that much time, but—"

"I've already hired many investigators," Sasha interrupted glumly. That was how she'd ended up in Phoenix. It had cost her one-hundred and fifty-five dollars to learn that her father had supposedly moved from Springfield, Missouri, to the desert town to work on a suburban weekly newspaper. Unfortunately, the lead had proven to be a dead end. One more in a very long string.

"Besides, I don't have the money necessary—"

"Don't worry about that," Jake said. "We'll take up a collection at the station. All the guys will be glad to pitch in."

"A P.I. isn't the answer," Mitch said suddenly, breaking into the conversation for the first time.

"You don't know that," Glory snapped. "That detective I hired last year to track down my second ex managed to get me five years back child support."

"It also took two months," Mitch reminded her. "And you had your ex-husband's social security number, which made it a helluva lot easier." He shook his head. "Unfortunately, Sasha's right. There's not enough time."

Glory's face was a stony mask. "We can't let them send her back. Her mother's dead. She doesn't have any family there anymore. She'll be all alone."

"I wasn't talking about letting her be deported."

Although Sasha was mildly annoyed that they'd begun talking about her as if she were no longer in the diner, she couldn't help being curious.

She slowly lifted her eyes to his. "I don't understand."

"The answer's obvious. And simple."

Glory lifted a dark brow. "So why don't you share it with us, hotshot?" she said, calling him by the name that had appeared in all those newspaper headlines.

"Sasha needs to marry a U.S. citizen. That way, she'll get her green card."

Sasha's hopes, which had soared when Mitch had suggested he had the solution to her dilemma, plummeted. Her shoulders sagged. He might as well have suggested she discover the Lost Dutchman's gold mine that was supposedly hidden somewhere in the nearby Superstition mountains while she was at it.

"As much as I appreciate your suggestion," she said with a tired sigh, "there is one little problem. I do not know anyone who would marry me."

"Of course you do."

Mitch heard the fatal words come out of his mouth and knew he was sunk. Although he'd tried to resist the idea as he'd listened to Sasha's painfully told story, he could feel himself about to take yet another headlong plunge into trouble.

Mitch wondered what deep-seated inner flaw he possessed that made it impossible for him to resist putting on his tarnished suit of armor.

He remembered a serial killer a few years back who wrote letters to newspapers all around the country that always began "Stop me before I kill again."

Perhaps he should have little cards printed to hand out at times like this; cards that read "Stop me before I help again."

Knowing he was about to make the biggest mistake of his life, but unable to resist, Mitch flashed the smile that had graced the cover of *Newsweek* and had so charmed Kathie

Lee—the cocky male grin that had the power to melt Sasha's heart.

Leaning down, he rubbed his fingertips lightly along the lines furrowing her brow, a gesture Sasha found wonderful and unnervingly intimate at the same time. "You know me," he said.

3

SASHA COULDN'T SPEAK, couldn't think. She was certain that what she'd heard was a joke. Or a wild hallucination born of stress and her subconscious desires.

"Well?" Mitch said when she didn't immediately answer. "What do you say?"

Sasha stared at him. Hope fluttered its delicate hummingbird wings in her breast, even as her mind assured her she must have misunderstood.

"I don't understand," she said, looking desperately at Jake and Glory for assistance.

Jake shrugged and continued to stare at his wife's brother, while Glory burst out laughing. "It may not have been the most romantic proposal in the world, Sasha, honey, but I do believe hotshot here just asked you to marry him."

"Marry?" She turned back to him, her eyes wide and disbelieving. "This is true, Mitch? You wish to marry me?"

"It wouldn't be a real marriage," he said quickly, ignoring Glory's easily heard muttered grunt of disapproval. "It would only be a legal maneuver to buy time for you to find your father."

"Now that's being real gentlemanly." Jake shook his head in disgust.

Mitch turned on him. "At least I came up with a solution. Which is more than you managed to do."

"Gotta point there," Jake agreed. "Of course, gettin' married to your sister kinda took me out of the matrimonial sweepstakes." The laughter left his eyes as he looked from Mitch to Sasha, then back to Mitch. "You know," he murmured, rubbing his square chin, "it could work, I suppose."

His gaze was warm and encouraging as it moved slowly over Sasha's tearstained face. "The hardest part, the way I see it, would be living under the same roof with you, hotshot." He winked at Sasha. "Not many women consider Jockey briefs hanging on the doorknob a decorating plus."

Sasha was more confused than ever. If she'd understood correctly, and she believed she had, Mitch was suggesting nothing more than a legal ploy to keep the nasty immigration officer at bay until she could find her father and prove her citizenship.

These things were done all the time. She knew of girls from St. Petersburg who had entered into similar agreements with men from Europe and the United States. Such marriages had nothing to do with romance. Or with love.

"We would live together?"

"No!" Mitch shouted.

"Yes!" Glory said at exactly the same moment.

Jake chuckled, seeming to enjoy his brother-in-law's discomfort and said nothing.

"If you two kids do try to pull this off, you're going to have to make it look like a real marriage," Glory warned. "I saw a report on '20/20' a couple weeks ago, showing how, because of the upcoming election and all the illegal alien arguments, the government is starting to crack down on green card marriages.

"That weasel Potter down at immigration isn't going to be satisfied with any convenient piece of paper signed by some Phoenix justice of the peace. He's going to want to make sure you two are actually living as man and wife.''

Hell, she was right. Mitch had seen the same report himself. He'd been over at Meredith's, and although it certainly wasn't the way he'd planned to spend an intimate Friday night with the sexy reporter, she'd appeared briefly in the segment anchored by John Stossel, so of course they'd both had to watch.

Meredith. Mitch cursed inwardly as he wondered what Meredith was going to say when she discovered her man of the moment had run off and gotten married. If only he'd taken the time to run the errant thought through his brain before letting it come out of his damn mouth. But, no. Once again, he'd gone charging into the breach, the same way he'd rushed into that burning building and ended up a media hero.

One of these days, Mitch told himself glumly, he really was going to have to learn self-restraint.

Sasha had never seen Mitch do anything but smile. Even after fighting a blazing, four-alarm fire in the blistering desert heat, when he was covered with soot and sweat, he could still flash her a devastating grin designed to turn any woman to butter.

But at this moment his handsome face was grim, telling her that he was already having regrets. In fact, she thought, he looked a great deal like a Siberian wolf who'd just stumbled into a trap and would be willing to chew his leg off, if necessary, to escape.

That being the case, although she desperately longed to say yes, if only to forestall her deportation to Russia, Sasha knew what she must do. Mitch had done a gracious and generous thing, a heroic thing, by asking her to marry him. Now she must be equally as honorable and refuse.

She swallowed her disappointment and tried to keep her lips from trembling. "As much as I appreciate your offer, Mitch, I can't allow you to ruin your life for me."

There it was, Mitch told himself. The escape hatch. All he had to do was walk through it and he'd be home free.

But then Sasha would be on her way back to a homeland where she had no home.

"I wouldn't be ruining my life." *Terrific, Cudahy,* he blasted himself. *Why don't you just dig the hole even deeper?* She was willing to let him off the hook, so why couldn't he just wiggle free? Like any sensible, sane person would do?

"Sure, marriage might prove a bit inconvenient, but it isn't going to last all that long. Just until we locate your father and you can prove your claim of citizenship."

Sasha turned toward the others, seeking advice. "Jake— Glory? What do you think of Mitch's idea?"

"I think you should do it," they said together.

She bit her lip and stared out the window again at the shiny red fire truck, remembering how wonderfully dashing Mitch had looked leaping down from the back of the truck with that lethal-looking ax in his strong dark hands, come to save her by stopping the diner from going up in flames.

To be married to this man would be a dream come true. Even if it wasn't a real marriage, what could it hurt to pretend? Just a little.

And it would definitely solve her problem with Potter. When the image of the sour-faced government official popped into her mind, Sasha made her decision.

"All right, Mitch." She turned back toward him, her expression as grave as her thoughts. "I will marry you."

Although Mitch knew it was his imagination, he was sure he could hear a door close and the lock click behind him.

After a brief discussion, they scheduled the wedding for Saturday night after Mitch's shift ended. At his suggestion, it was decided that they'd drive to Laughlin, Nevada, a small gambling town situated on the banks of the Colorado River across the border from Arizona.

"We can get the deed done there," Mitch promised, "then be home before lunchtime Sunday."

It would be, he assured her, quick and efficient. It also did not escape Sasha's notice that he didn't suggest that anyone else in his family be present for the ceremony.

There was a reason for that. Knowing how his mother wanted him to "find a nice girl and settle down," Mitch purposely decided not to tell her about the plan. Although he'd hoped that Katie and Jake's new baby would take the heat off him for a while, she was continually informing him that it was his responsibility to ensure the Cudahy name be carried on into another generation. He definitely didn't want to get her hopes up with this fake wedding.

MITCH WAS three hours late arriving at her rooming house the night they were to get married.

Sasha had given notice that she would be moving out, had packed her meager belongings and then had waited worriedly, afraid he'd changed his mind.

"Sorry," he said, "there was a fire in a warehouse. I couldn't get away."

"I was worried."

"That I wasn't going to come?"

"No." As he watched the soft color bloom in her cheeks, Mitch tried to remember the last time he'd been with a woman capable of blushing. "Well, maybe I did worry for just a little while that you'd changed your mind," she confessed. "But mostly I was worried about you. When I heard about the fire on the radio, I feared you would be hurt."

"Never happen," he said with the same bravado that allowed him to eat smoke for a living. "Well, I suppose we may as well get this show on the road."

Conversation on the drive to Nevada was stilted. And the mood was decidedly less than upbeat. In fact, Sasha had seen a movie where an old Western outlaw had gone to his hanging with more enthusiasm than Mitch showed for his upcoming marriage.

Like most little girls the world over, Sasha had dreamed of her wedding day. And although that dream had changed as she'd left her childhood behind her, the one thing that had remained constant was the fact that her groom would be handsome. And that he would love her.

Absolutely.

Forever.

Well, Sasha considered, giving a soft, rippling little sigh, at least one of those things would be true. Although Mitch didn't love her, he would certainly make a handsome groom. Even better than any of her romantic fantasies.

Once in Laughlin, the proceedings moved fast and efficiently, just as Mitch had promised.

"So far, so good," he said with feigned enthusiasm as they filled out the paperwork. Sasha had seemed down in the dumps since he'd shown up at her apartment and he doubted she'd said two words during the drive from Phoenix.

Her sad little frown kept her from looking much like a glowing bride-to-be. Conveniently forgetting that he'd been the one to insist this wasn't going to be a real marriage, Mitch figured the lady could at least try to appear a little enthusiastic about the idea.

Didn't she realize more than one woman in Phoenix would be tickled pink to receive a proposal from all-American hero Mitch Cudahy? Hell, after appearing on

"Good Morning America" and "Ricki Lake," he'd gotten marriage proposals from interested females as far away as Anchorage, Alaska. He'd even received a candygram—accompanied by her centerfold photo—from a former *Playboy* Miss July.

Mitch handed over his Visa card to the clerk. They waited while the charges were run through the machine, then carried the forms next door to the Chapel of Love.

It was then things got interesting.

"I don't believe this!" Mitch stared in horror at the overweight man wearing a white jumpsuit.

"Mitch?" Sasha's eyes widened. It was just like her favorite American film! "This is an Elvis person, yes? Like in the movie, *Honeymoon in Vegas.*"

"That's right, honeybun," the rotund man answered boisterously before Mitch had a chance to respond. He had to raise his voice to be heard over an enthusiastic rendition of "All Shook Up" coming from the oversize speakers hanging on all four walls of the room.

"I'm Elvis Presley." He flashed a bold, confident grin as he held out a fleshy hand weighted down with diamond rings. "Had my name legally changed for my profession."

"You thought it would help your ministerial business to be named after a dead singer?" Mitch asked.

"Not just any old run-of-the-mill singer, boy. The King." He gave Sasha a broad smile. "I'm an Elvis impersonator, all right, little lady. Just like in that nifty movie, only I'm too old and too chicken to go jumping out of airplanes. And aren't you the prettiest little bride I've married all day?"

Mitch had been regretting his decision to propose since he'd first heard the words coming out of his mouth. There was no way he was going to go through with a farce like this.

"We're getting out of here." He grabbed hold of Sasha's hand and began to pull her out the door.

To his surprise, she dug in her high heels.

"Sasha?" Impatience surged as she held her ground. "What's wrong now?"

"Nothing is wrong, Mitch." The way she was looking at the ridiculously clad minister reminded him of the way Dane, the six-year-old boy assigned to him in the Big Brother program, looked at the latest Power Ranger action figure in the toy store window. "This is wonderful!"

"It's ridiculous, is what it is," he corrected gruffly, immensely relieved that none of the guys from Ladder Company No. 13 were here to witness this debacle. "Let's go. There's gotta be another minister somewhere in town."

"But, Mitch—"

"The little lady seems real happy right where she is," the minister observed in a deep Tennessee drawl.

"When you suggested coming to Laughlin, I never expected anything like this, Mitch," Sasha said.

"That makes two of us."

"It is so exciting. And romantic," she wheedled prettily. "We would never have anything so wonderful like this back in Russia. Ever since I was a little girl, I have dreamed of such a wedding."

"You dreamed of getting married by an old fat Elvis?" Realizing that he'd just insulted the minister, he said, "Sorry. I didn't mean that personally."

"No offense taken," the man said cheerfully as the Muzak system segued into "Don't Be Cruel." "And, hell, I know I'm old and fat. But the original Elvis was carrying a few extra pounds, too, at the end. So the way I figure it, if it was good enough for the King, it's good enough for me."

"Please, Mitch." Sasha removed her hand from his iron grip and placed it on his arm. "We've already paid for the license. This nice man is ready to marry us—"

"Nothin' I'd like better than to unite you two lovebirds in holy matrimony," the minister broke in.

"See." She pressed her case. "Doesn't it make sense to exchange our vows here? Instead of driving all over town looking for a substitute minister? Or perhaps having to go all the way to Las Vegas?"

"Aw, hell." He wondered what kind of man that unyielding immigration officer was to be able to refuse this woman anything. Obviously Donald O. Potter had a heart of stone. "Okay. Here's the deal... If I agree to go along with this ridiculous circus, you have to promise never to tell Jake, or Glory, or anyone else we know."

"I promise." Her slender fingers squeezed his forearm with surprising strength. "It will be our secret. But, Mitch, it would make me so very, very happy."

Mitch didn't know which one of them was crazier. The old guy in the rhinestone-covered polyester jumpsuit with about a quart of Valvoline in his hair; Sasha for wanting to get married by an Elvis impersonator—and not a very good one, at that, or himself for even considering going along with the cockeyed scheme.

Looking down into her warm, brown, hopeful eyes, he felt himself giving in again. "All right," he agreed with a deep, resigned sigh. "If it's really what you want."

"Oh, thank you!" Excitedly, she flung her arms around his neck and kissed him.

At the first touch of her mouth, Mitch experienced a momentary surprise. Then, as her silky lips melded into his and her wondrous breasts pressed enticingly against his chest, he decided not to think of all the reasons why this was a big mistake and dove headlong into the kiss.

Her generous mouth was as soft as it looked. But much, much, warmer. Mitch had given the matter a great deal of thought since that fatal day when, after putting out the fire in the diner, he'd looked up to see her standing in the doorway, pale as a wraith and trembling. Her lips had quivered in a way that practically begged for a man to kiss away her fears, and Mitch had suspected that Sasha's mouth would be sweet. And innocent.

Innocent, it definitely was. From the way she kept her lips pressed tightly together, he suspected she had not been kissed very often. Or very well. And yet even with her obvious lack of experience, her kiss was far more potent than even he, who'd certainly known more than his share of women, could have imagined.

The dark, rich taste of her seeped into his mouth, into his blood, causing it to burn. When he caught her full lower lip between his teeth, her resultant shudder sent all that heated blood shooting south, below his belt.

Even knowing that such a scenario was impossible, Sasha had dreamed of this moment innumerable times over the past weeks. But never could she have imagined the power of Mitch's kiss. Her head filled with sounds like the roaring winds of a hurricane, and her body began to glow as if somehow the sun had fallen from the sky and entered her bloodstream through Mitch's hot, hungry mouth.

And then, just like that, it was over.

The strong, dark hands that had created such heat as they'd roamed up and down her back, settled at her waist as Mitch put her away from him. He was looking down at her, but his shuttered gaze gave Sasha no inkling of what he was thinking.

"Well, we've wasted enough time," he said. He had no way of knowing how his brusque words stung Sasha who was still caught up in the glory of that wondrous kiss.

"I'd say so," the minister said with a bold laugh that made his belly shake and the rhinestones flash. "Because if there was ever a couple ready for a honeymoon, I'd say it was you two."

At the mention of a honeymoon, Sasha blushed. As Mitch's body continued to throb, on cue, the King began belting out "A Big Hunk O' Love."

"So, you two kids got a ring?"

Mitch cursed. "I forgot all about a ring."

"It's all right," Sasha said quickly. Her brave little smile only served to make him more irritated at the entire situation. And even more, at himself. "I do not need a ring."

"Maybe you don't. But I'll bet Potter will."

"Oh." She sighed as she envisioned the grim immigration officer. "I suppose you're right."

Elvis rubbed his beefy hands together with robust satisfaction. "You're in luck. Because I just happen to have a real nice selection right here."

He pulled a black velvet tray out of a drawer beneath the counter. The rings ranged from a simple silver band to a sparkling diamond the size of Vermont.

Mitch scanned the tray, his gaze settling on a gleaming woven gold ring boasting a small but good quality diamond. "How about this one?"

"That's a dandy choice," Elvis agreed. "It's one of my most popular styles."

"Sasha?" He held the ring out to her. "What do you think?"

What did she think? She thought the delicate gold mesh was the loveliest thing she'd ever seen. And the diamond glittered like a midnight star! She also worried he couldn't afford such a glorious piece of jewelry on his modest civil servant's salary.

"It's very pretty." With effort, she dragged her eyes back to the tray. "But this one will be fine." She pointed to a thin, plain silver band.

"That'd be nice, too," Elvis said agreeably. But with less gusto, Mitch noticed. And for good reason. The silver ring practically shouted "Cheapskate budget special."

"I like this one." Telling himself that he had a reputation to protect, that he didn't want his new bride returning to Phoenix and showing off that miserably mediocre excuse for a wedding band, he held his ground. "Let's try it on."

Sasha obediently held out her hand, embarrassed by the way it was trembling.

"Don't worry about the shakes, honeybun," Elvis said reassuringly. "I've done over a thousand marriages and, believe me, every one of those brides-to-be had prewedding nerves."

Sasha thought that could well be true. But, of course, she was not really a bride. So why was she so nervous?

"It fits!" The ring slid onto her finger so easily it could have been made with her in mind. She held it out, admiring the gleam of the yellow gold, the flash of the diamond.

"Okay, that's it, then." Mitch dug his billfold out of his jeans and again handed over his Visa card.

"How about flowers?" Elvis asked.

An instantaneous flash of pleasure lit Sasha's dark eyes. When it was just as quickly extinguished, Mitch realized that she was trying to be frugal on his account.

"Can't get married without flowers," he said.

As he watched Sasha dip her head and breathe in the sweet scent of carnations, Mitch remembered the elaborate preparations for his sister's wedding to Jake. Katie had driven everyone crazy, insisting the formal ceremony live up to the one she'd always dreamed of.

Although at the time he'd found her behavior incomprehensible, now he began to realize that wedding fantasies were apparently one thing all females—from Phoenix to St. Petersburg—had in common.

"Is that it?" His irritation at himself for being miserly at a time like this made his voice harsher than he'd meant it to be.

Sasha jumped, dropping the edge of the lovely short white lace veil she'd been fingering. "You have already bought more than enough, Mitch. Truly."

"Fine." He turned to the minister. "Let's do it."

"You got it, young fella. Soon as I call my wife, Annie, so she can be a witness." He tapped on a small bell and a door behind him opened and out came a tall, curvaceous redhead.

"Don't tell me," Mitch groaned as he recognized the woman's uncanny resemblance to Ann Margaret. *"Viva Las Vegas."*

"Got it on the first try." Elvis grinned conspiratorially.

If he ever got married again—which he had no intention of doing—Mitch vowed he was going to insist on a civil ceremony at the Phoenix courthouse.

Mitch and Sasha followed Elvis and his wife into an adjoining room where an ivory satin runner led to a small altar set up in front of a white satin curtain. On the altar, a vase in the shape of the young Elvis holding a guitar, held a fragrant assortment of fresh gladioli.

"Sorry, little lady," Elvis said, "I can understand how you probably hate to part with it, but I'm going to have to ask you to give me that ring. Just for a few minutes."

Sasha took the diamond ring from her finger, experiencing a sense of loss as she handed it over.

"All right," he said with robust satisfaction, "it's time for the show! Sasha, honey, you start at the door and walk toward your fella, while Annie and I sing your wedding march."

"Is that really necessary?" Mitch asked.

This was already dragging on a lot longer than planned. And, although he kept telling himself that it wasn't real, despite the surrealistic aspect of the ceremony, it still felt too much like a wedding for comfort.

"All brides dream of walking up the aisle, don't they, honey?" the older woman said to Sasha.

"I would like that very much," she agreed, casting a hesitant glance Mitch's way. "But if Mitch would rather just begin, that would be all right with me, as well."

Damn. She'd gotten that whipped cocker spaniel look in her eyes again. "We're wasting time arguing," Mitch said. "Why don't you just walk up the aisle?"

"Thank you, Mitch!"

Once again that warm pleasure flooded her eyes, making him feel like the grinch who'd tried to steal Sasha's wedding.

Holding the overpriced flowers in her hands, she walked slowly up the white satin runner toward him, while Elvis and Annie sang a medley of "Love Me Tender," which Mitch had to admit wasn't half bad.

As Mitch watched her approach, he realized that somehow, even in her ugly-as-sin severe black suit and starched white blouse, Sasha was still lovely.

When she reached Mitch's side, Elvis pulled a white satin cord. The curtain behind the altar opened, revealing a large-screen television. A moment later the wedding scene from *Blue Hawaii* flashed onto the oversize screen and the deep tones of the King crooning "The Hawaiian Wedding Song" filled the room.

"Oh, Mitch, isn't it romantic!" Sasha clapped her hands in pleasure.

Immensely grateful that Jake wasn't there, Mitch shook his head and imagined his brother-in-law telling this story at the firehouse. Hell, he'd never be able to live it down.

"Dearly beloved," Elvis began, raising his voice to be heard over the ballad.

The images on the television screen began to shimmer. As the music swelled, the vaguely familiar words of the wedding ceremony began to sound like a dull roar in Mitch's ears.

Sweat beaded on his forehead and above his upper lip. As he heard Sasha promise to take him as her lawfully wedded husband, his legs began to shake. But not from fear, Mitch assured himself, stiffening his knees as he managed to shove the ring onto her outstretched finger.

He was a smoke eater. A hero. Guys like him lived on the edge; they weren't afraid of anything.

Elvis turned toward him. "And do you, Mitchel Dylan Cudahy, take this woman, Sasha Mikhailova, for your lawfully wedded wife?"

Her face, as she looked up at him, appeared concerned. Mitch straightened his spine and took a deep breath.

"To love and to honor." Little white spots began to dance in front of his eyes. "For richer or poorer." Blinded by the sweat pouring from his brow, Mitch wiped his forehead with a quick swipe with the back of his hand. "In sickness and in health. For as long as you both shall live."

"I do," Mitch managed.

He'd barely croaked out the response before he pitched forward, landing facedown at Sasha's feet.

"Mitch!" As the King wrapped up the song to his movie bride, Sasha sank to her knees beside her groom. Heedless of the blood that was pouring from his nose, darkening his shirt, she gathered Mitch into her arms.

Annie, apparently accustomed to nervous grooms passing out, calmly plucked the gladioli out of the vase, then tossed the water into Mitch's face.

Mitch sputtered, shaking his head like the ladder company's Dalmatian who'd just had a fire hose turned on him.

As he regained consciousness, he heard Elvis boomingly proclaim, ''By the power invested in me by the State of Nevada—and the King of Rock and Roll—I now pronounce you husband and wife!''

4

"ARE YOU SURE you're all right?" Sasha asked with concern as they walked out into the blinding sun.

"I'm fine," Mitch snapped from between clenched teeth. "Why wouldn't I be? I was up nearly the whole damn night fighting a two-alarm blaze, I drove halfway across the damn desert, I practically maxed out my credit card to get married by some fat old Elvis impersonator and his crazy redheaded wife, and then, to top if off, I passed out and broke my nose."

"The doctor Elvis called to the chapel said it is not broken," she reminded him quietly. Sasha had never seen Mitch so angry. Obviously he was already regretting this false marriage.

"The guy was probably a quack," Mitch growled as he opened the passenger door of the Mustang.

Not wanting to risk angering him further by arguing that the doctor had seemed quite competent, Sasha didn't answer. Every atom in his body was radiating with irritation as he came around the front of the red convertible, yanked open the door and flung himself into the bucket seat beside her.

Tears stung behind her lids. Refusing to humiliate herself by crying again in front of him, Sasha bit her lip.

He jammed the key into the ignition and turned it.

Instead of the familiar purr of the engine coming to life, there was only a faint click.

Mitch cursed.

Then twisted the key again.

Again, nothing.

"Dammit!" He hit the steering wheel with the heel of his hand. "This will definitely go down in history as the worst damn day of my life!"

That did it!

Sasha had tried to stay cheerful during the long drive to the desert gambling town, even when Mitch hadn't bothered to say more than two gruff words to her.

She'd ignored his less-than-enthusiastic response to a wedding, that while not exactly a fairy-tale dream ceremony, was at least more colorful than the dreary civil procedure she'd been expecting.

She hadn't even complained about his blood stains all over her only decent suit.

But to have him behave as if he was blaming her for his car not starting was the final straw!

Bursting into the furious tears she'd tried to forestall, she flung open the passenger door and went marching off across the parking lot.

"Aw, hell." Mitch lowered his forehead to the steering wheel, ignoring the painful lump that was forming there. He closed his eyes and took a deep breath. Then, calling himself every kind of bastard, he took off after his bride.

Despite her head start, Mitch quickly caught up with her and grabbed hold of her arm. "Dammit, Sasha—"

"Let go of me!" She shook free and kept on walking.

"Look, I'm sorry."

No answer.

"It's just that it's been a lousy few days," he tried again.

"You think you have had bad days?" She spun around, her eyes shooting furious sparks. "Let me tell you, Mitch Cudahy—" she began, shoving her finger in his chest, then went off on a furious stream of Russian.

Although he couldn't understand a word she was shouting at him, Mitch suspected that she wasn't being complimentary.

"Would you mind very much speaking English so I at least understand you?"

She glared at him. "This has not exactly been wonderful for me, either! I have been threatened with deportation by a dreadful man who would like nothing more than to send me back to Russia, made to believe that I'd been stood up at the altar when you did not arrive at the time you promised—"

"I explained about that," Mitch reminded her. "It wasn't my fault that warehouse caught on fire ten minutes before the end of my shift. What was I supposed to do? Tell the captain that I was sorry, but I couldn't climb on the damn truck because I had to get married?"

She raised her chin haughtily. "I would appreciate it very much if you did not continually interrupt while I am speaking."

"I was just trying to make a point. And you're not exactly speaking, sweetheart, you're shouting."

Knowing he did not mean the word sweetheart as an endearment, Sasha let loose with another heated barrage of Russian.

"And I am not shouting!" she finished in heavily accented English.

Of course she was. Sasha paused and took a deep, calming breath.

Watching her shoulders begin to shake, Mitch readied himself for another onslaught of feminine tears.

"I am not shouting," she said with a surprising giggle that lit up her eyes and moved something very elemental—and disconcerting—inside him. "I am a calm person. I never shout."

Mitch felt his own lips curving into a reluctant smile. "Of course you don't. Just like I'm never in a bad mood."

Their individual anger cooled like flames hit with a stream of water from one of Mitch's fire hoses. This time when he took hold of her hand, she did not pull away.

"I'm sorry, Sasha. I overreacted."

"No," she sighed, unhappy that she'd created such a scene when all he'd been trying to do was help, "it is I who should apologize. After all, you were kind enough to offer to marry me."

Mitch didn't want to be reminded of his unfortunate tendency to rush into situations where any self-respecting angel would hesitate to tread.

"How about we just start over?"

"You want to go back and do our Elvis wedding again?"

Her eyes twinkled with laughter, her smiling lips were full and inviting, suddenly reminding Mitch that by passing out, he'd missed the traditional ending to the wedding ceremony.

Unfortunately, as memories of their earlier shared kiss flashed hotly through his mind, he decided kissing Sasha in a public parking lot was more of a risk than he was willing to take. Even in a town built on gambling.

"We might as well get a hotel room," he said. "Then I'll call the auto club."

"A hotel room? But I thought you wanted to return to Phoenix right after the wedding."

"We can't go anywhere until we get a new starter. It's Sunday. There won't be any place open that can put one in until tomorrow. Looks like we're stuck here for the night."

"Oh." The idea of spending the night in a hotel room with Mitch was as terrifying as it was thrilling. "This will cost more money, yes?"

"Don't worry about it."

With their fingers laced together, they walked back to the car, retrieved their things and walked to the hotel next door.

"What do you mean, you're all booked up?" Mitch asked incredulously.

"Exactly that." The man behind the registration desk shrugged. "All our rooms are taken."

"Fine. We'll just go to another hotel."

"Don't think you'll have much luck anywhere else," the clerk said laconically. "There's an international Shriner's convention this weekend. And a championship boxing match at the Flamingo."

"Don't worry," Mitch assured Sasha as they walked out of the gilt and marble lobby into the blinding Nevada sunshine, "there's got to be something available."

Thirty minutes later he was ready to concede defeat. "I'll give you whatever you want if you will only find us a room," he said, staggering up to the reception desk of the sixth hotel they'd tried.

Sasha's luggage, which had not seemed heavy in the beginning, now felt like a ton of bricks. "All my money, my credit cards, my firstborn child. Anything you ask for. It's yours."

The sleek blonde behind the desk eyed Mitch with unsuppressed amusement. "You're in luck. We've just had a cancellation."

"Bless you." If the counter hadn't been between them, Mitch would have kissed her. Right on her glossy pink lips.

"A couple from Wichita booked the honeymoon suite six weeks ago," the reservations clerk revealed. "Then apparently, they got in a fight over which Elvis song to play at the ceremony, and the bride stormed out of the chapel and took a cab to the airport. The groom just called to cancel the room.''

Mitch exchanged a look with Sasha, who was struggling to keep a straight face. "They should have gone with 'The Hawaiian Wedding Song.'"

"It worked for me and my husband when Elvis married us last year," the clerk agreed cheerfully. "But apparently when the groom-to-be insisted on 'Jailhouse Rock,' the bride took that as a metaphor for how he viewed their marriage, and blew up."

She began tapping on the computer keyboard. "The suite's all ready. Will you be paying with a credit card?"

"Why not?" Mitch said, pulling out the gold card yet again.

Five minutes later they were alone in a vast suite that appeared to have been designed by a crazed cupid and cost him nearly two week's pay. Mitch decided that whoever had said two could live as cheaply as one obviously hadn't eloped to Laughlin, Nevada, during a Shriner's convention.

"Goodness," Sasha said, staring at the round bed set on a burgundy fabric-covered platform, surrounded by gilded pillars, covered with a pink and velvet spread and strewn with pillows. "I had no idea they made waterbeds so large. Even in America." In some of the apartments she'd been in St. Petersburg, entire families would undoubtedly be expected to share such an expansive bed.

She glanced up at the ceiling. "And what a strange place for a mirror."

She looked a mess, Sasha decided regretfully. Her hair was windblown, her makeup had melted, she'd chewed her lipstick off and the blood on the front of her white blouse had dried to an unattractive rust color. At least she wouldn't have to worry about Mitch kissing her again. Because, looking as rumpled as she did, she was definitely not the least bit appealing.

"Not so strange," Mitch said, putting her suitcases beside the bed. "Given the fact that this is the honeymoon suite."

"I still do not understand...oh." Color flooded into her face as comprehension dawned.

"Oh," he mimicked with a quick grin, once again enjoying that soft pink color brightening her cheeks. She was so damn pretty. Her hair was a dark froth around her shoulders, and although she'd chewed off her lipstick, her lips were a rich rosy hue that, even though he knew it would be playing with fire, made him want to kiss her senseless. "I guess it's a good thing that this wedding of ours isn't real."

He tamped down an errant image of Sasha, lying nude on satin sheets, her hair spread out on the pillow, as she held her arms out to her lover, her husband.

"A very good thing," she agreed, having to force the words past the lump that had suddenly taken residence in her throat.

Unbidden, a mental picture flashed though her mind, of Mitch's muscular back and firm buttocks reflected in the overhead mirror as his lips blazed a hot trail down her naked body.

Their eyes met in the mirror and held. Silence settled over them as each was unwillingly drawn into a sensual fantasy to which neither was prepared to admit.

"Well." Mitch cleared his throat and dragged his gaze away to the gilded dresser that looked like it could have come straight from Versailles. Atop the dresser, on a silver tray, was a bottle of champagne and a box of Belgian chocolates wrapped in gold foil paper and tied with a red satin ribbon.

"I'd better call the auto club and arrange for someone to come out first thing tomorrow morning."

It was not Mitch's first choice. What he wanted to do was to pop that cork, ply his bride with champagne and spend the rest of the day feeding her chocolates and making love.

"Yes." It was barely a whisper.

"If you want, you can freshen up. Then we'll see about getting something to eat. We can go out, if you'd like. Or maybe you'd rather call room service."

"They will bring our dinner to our room?"

"All you have to do is ask." *And pay through the nose,* Mitch thought but didn't say. He'd already gone so far over budget, he wasn't about to start quibbling about extra costs now.

"That sounds very nice." Sasha thought about the temptations of staying here so close to this ridiculously sensual bed with a man who'd played a starring role in her fantasies since she'd first seen him.

"But, perhaps, if you don't mind, we could go out?" she suggested. "I saw a coffee shop next to the lobby."

"Good idea." Relief and regret flooded through Mitch; relief that she'd suggested getting them out of this gilded love nest, away from temptation, regret that he wouldn't be making love to her on the terrifically sexy bed.

Sasha might be able to resist the oversize waterbed, but the pink-tiled, heart-shaped Jacuzzi bathtub was another matter. Seemingly as deep as a lake, and nearly large enough to swim laps in, she decided American plumbing was one of the seven wonders of the world.

"Mitch?" she called out through the open bathroom door, "would you mind very much if I took the time for a bath?"

"Suit yourself," he answered as the recorded message assured him that his call was important and thanked him for his patience. "I have the feeling I'm going to be on hold for a long time."

When she spotted the crystal jars of bath salts lining the pink rim of the enormous tub, Sasha considered that if the angry bride had known what she was passing up, perhaps she wouldn't have been so quick to reject her groom's choice of music.

Thirty minutes later, the perfumed, bubbling water had soothed Sasha's exhaustion and her nerves. As she wrapped the thick, terry bath sheet around her body, she couldn't remember ever feeling so relaxed.

Although she suspected dining in such a splendid hotel would require something equally dazzling, her luggage did not offer a plethora of chic outfits. That being the case, she opted for a short denim skirt and a red cotton blouse with handstitched embroidery along the peasant neckline, hoping she wouldn't embarrass Mitch too badly.

Then she brushed her hair in an attempt to subdue her wild waves. She was, as usual, unsuccessful. Her thick hair remained as unruly as ever, making Sasha envy the sleek blond bobs favored by Mitch's usual women.

Reminding herself that she was not one of Mitch's women—nor was she likely to ever be one—she left the bedroom.

Having spent the previous night fighting a fire had obviously caught up with Mitch. He was sprawled on his back on the sofa, sound asleep, giving Sasha the opportunity to study him undetected. Her gaze drank in the thick curly eyelashes that seemed such a waste on a man, the slightly pug nose, the full, firmly cut lips, the square, pugnacious chin.

His chest rose and fell with each slow breath and as she remembered how it had felt against her breasts, hard as marble but so much warmer, a disturbing heat flowed through her. Her eyes continued their stolen tour, taking in his lean hips, his long legs.

When she found herself wanting to lie down beside him, Sasha knew it was time to leave.

Not wanting him to think she'd run away again, she took the time to write a note on the hotel stationery. Then she quickly left the honeymoon suite.

She was on the way to the coffee shop when the noise from an adjoining room made her realize she was passing the casino. Curious, she glanced inside. It was exactly like *Honeymoon in Vegas*!

Hand-cut prisms on the crystal chandeliers sparkled from the ceiling, murals had been painted on the walls between gilded pillars, the carpet underfoot was burgundy and gold. Slot machines clattered and conversation hummed, punctuated periodically by shouts of excitement and cries of despair.

Sasha found it all enthralling. So enthralling, in fact, she couldn't resist venturing inside.

"Here you go, little lady." A man wearing a fez stood up and handed her a large silver coin. "I've been sitting on this stool for the past hour and haven't won a blessed thing. Perhaps you'll have better luck."

"Luck?" Sasha glanced down at the coin. She had been in America a year and had never seen such a denomination. "I do not understand."

"At the slots." His dark eyes narrowed as he studied her closer. "You're not from around here."

"No. I am from Phoenix, Arizona."

"Before that."

"Oh." She nodded. "I came to America from St. Petersburg, Russia."

It was his turn to nod. "That's why you sound like Natasha."

"Natasha is a common name in Russia," she said with another brief nod. "But I am called Sasha."

"Now isn't that a right pretty name, too?" he said. "But I was talking about Natasha from the TV show. You know, the Saturday morning cartoons? Bullwinkle? Rocky? Moose and Squirrel?"

He could have been speaking Transylvanian. She stared mutely at him, trying to decode the unfamiliar references.

"Never mind," he said. "It's not important. So, Sasha, you want to try your luck?"

"I'm afraid my luck has not been very good lately," she admitted with a soft little sigh.

"Mine, either. Perhaps we can be each other's good luck charm. My name's Ben Houston, by the way. From Dallas, Texas, which doesn't make a lot of sense, I know, but I couldn't help where my pappy decided to settle. Old Sam Houston was a kin of mine."

Not understanding this reference, either, Sasha gave Ben Houston another longer, more judicial look. He was in his mid-fifties, with silver hair beneath the red-tasseled fez and friendly blue eyes. She could see nothing dangerous in his smiling gaze.

Besides, she reminded herself, it wasn't as if they were alone. The room was filled with people, all of whom seemed to be having a wonderfully carefree time. There was an energy here like nothing she'd ever felt.

It had been so long since Sasha had truly enjoyed herself, she found it impossible to resist the offer to do so now.

"I'm afraid you will have to teach me what to do. I have never gambled before."

"Sure you have. Life's a gamble. We risk getting run over by a bus every morning when we leave the house. And, hell, do you have any idea how many people are struck by lightning every year?"

"No."

"Neither do I. But it's a lot. The thing is, Sasha, honey, most days, we manage to beat the odds. Take my pap for instance. When he graduated from Texas A&M on the G.I. bill after World War Two, he was just another dirt-poor wildcatter with a degree in geology and a yen to get rich. Drilled twelve dusters before he hit lucky number thirteen. And never looked back."

Sasha was Russian enough to find such fatalism appealing. "I think I would like to try my luck, Mr. Houston," she decided.

"That's the girl! And the name's, Ben, honey. My daddy's Mr. Houston. Now let's get rid of this last unlucky damn dollar, then we'll decide what to play next."

Sasha put the coin in the slot he indicated, then pulled the lever beside the machine. The reels in the center of the machine spun around, too fast for her to follow the spinning pictures.

Then the first one stopped on number seven. The second one stopped on a seven, as well. Then the third.

Before Sasha could ask the man what happened, bells began to ring, the lights on the machine began flashing and her companion started slapping her on the back!

"Hot damn, sugar!" he whooped. "You won the jackpot!"

"The jackpot?" She had to shout to be heard over the deafening racket as coins started pouring into the tray. "The machine is broken, yes?" she asked as more and more silver dollars flowed into the tray.

"The machine is perfect, yes!" Ben corrected. "You won, Sasha. This is all yours! Hot damn, I knew a pretty little thing like you would change my luck!"

A crowd had gathered around her, applauding, shouting out encouragement as the money continued to flow from the machine like a sparkling silver waterfall. When it began flowing over the tray, someone handed her a foam cup. And then another. And another, and still the money continued to pour forth, almost faster than she could scoop it up.

A woman clad in a tuxedo shirt, very tight shorts and black mesh panty hose appeared with a tall green bottle and two tulip-shaped glasses.

"For you," she said, holding one of the glasses out to Sasha. "A gift from the management, with our congratulations."

Still confused, her hands filled with coins, Sasha looked over at her companion for guidance.

"It's champagne," Ben told her.

"Ah." She nodded. "*Shampahnskaye.* I know of this wine. But I have never tasted any." In Russia, the exorbitant cost had made it a drink only high party officials and government diplomats could afford.

"Now that's a real shame. Because pretty girls should always drink champagne." Ben took the glass and held it up to her mouth. "Drink up, honeybunch," he said encouragingly. "It's celebration time."

The shimmering gold wine was like nothing she'd ever tasted. It tickled her nose, even as it slid smoothly down her throat. "It tastes like laughter."

"You called that one right," Ben agreed, laughing heartily as he downed the contents of the other glass in one long swallow. "Come on, Sasha, let's go count your winnings."

She couldn't believe it. This couldn't be happening to her! Not even in America. Why, it hadn't even happened to Nicholas Cage in *Honeymoon in Vegas.* In that movie, she remembered, he'd lost all his money.

"Four thousand dollars?" she asked after the calculations had been completed.

"Four thousand, seven hundred and forty-eight dollars," Ben corrected.

"This is real?"

"About as real as you can get."

Sasha thought about what she could do with so much money. She could reimburse Mitch for all he'd spent on her behalf today—the ring, the flowers, the license, the wedding and the luxurious suite. She could pay it all back and still have money left over to hire another private detective to track down her father.

There was only one small problem.

She turned to Ben, who'd poured them both another glass of champagne. "This money belongs to you, Ben."

Startled, he choked on the champagne. After giving her a long look, he said, "You know, I think you mean that."

"Of course I do. It was your dollar I put into the machine. So this is rightfully your jackpot."

There was a murmur from the gathered crowd, as if everyone else was as surprised by her response as Ben was.

"That's not the way it works," he insisted. "I'd already given up on that fool machine when I gave you the dollar. You won it, Sasha. Fair and square. All four thousand, seven hundred and forty dollars of it."

"Forty-eight," she corrected absently. Her head was swimming from the sight of all that money, the excitement and the champagne.

"Forty-eight," he agreed with a rough, hearty bark of a laugh.

As generous as he seemed to be, Sasha could not help feeling guilty at the way his act of kindness was turning out. "Perhaps we could share."

"Honey, so long as the black gold keeps flowing back home, I've got so much money that my wife can't even break me with her damn daily shopping trips to Neiman

Marcus,'' he assured her. ''Gambling's best when it's done for fun, and I'm having more fun watching you win than I've had in a long time.'' He gave her another of those bold friendly grins that had her smiling back.

''So, you want to stop now? Or see if we can make this pile grow even higher?''

This was all new to Sasha, but even so, she knew that a sensible woman would stop now. She'd take her winnings and go back upstairs. Before she ended up like Nicholas Cage, broke and desperate.

But then another part of her, the part of her that had left her homeland and crossed an ocean to find a father everyone told her did not exist, the side of her that had married a man she barely knew, pushed aside the practical, careful Sasha.

''I think I would like to try to make it higher,'' she said recklessly.

As the onlookers cheered their approval, she allowed Ben to lead her over to a long table covered with green felt. There were numbers on the felt. And colors. And a black wheel. As she watched, a man in a tuxedo spun the wheel, causing a metal ball to bounce.

''This here is roulette,'' Ben said. ''You'd have better chances with blackjack, but this'll be easier for you to understand.''

The wheel stopped. A pile of colorful plastic chips was placed in front of her.

She looked up at Ben. ''Now what?''

''Choose a number.''

She shook her head as she stared at the wheel, suddenly all too aware that she was risking real money. ''There are too many.''

''No problem. Let's start with a color. Red or black.''

"Oh, that is easy. Red." The color of Mitch's shiny fire truck and his racy Mustang convertible.

She placed a chip on the spot Ben indicated, then held her breath as the banker spun the wheel and the ball started bouncing again.

Time seemed to pass in slow motion. Just when she thought she couldn't stand the suspense any longer, the wheel stopped and the ball bounced into the number ten slot.

"It is red!" she cried, clapping her hands. "This means I won, yes?"

"It means you won, yes," Ben agreed as the banker shoved her chip plus another one toward her. "Didn't I tell you we'd bring each other luck? Want to go again?"

"Yes." She put both chips on red again.

Ben followed her example, putting an enormous stack of his own plastic chips beside hers.

Feeling more daring than she'd ever felt before in her life, Sasha quickly took a smaller stack of her own chips and placed them on red, as well.

Then held her breath again as she waited for the spinning wheel to stop.

5

MITCH'S FIRST thought when he woke up to silence was that Sasha must have fallen asleep in the tub. A check of his watch revealed that he'd been out for two hours. If she was still in the water after all this time, she'd be as wrinkled as a prune.

Perhaps, he decided, she was taking a nap on that ridiculously sexy waterbed.

He pushed himself off the glove-soft leather sofa, finger combed his hair, ran his tongue over his teeth and wished he'd thought to at least pack a toothbrush. "Sasha?"

There was no answer. The only sound was the pounding beat of music drifting up from the floor below. It seemed that their expensive honeymoon suite in the exclusive tower area of the hotel was situated over a cocktail lounge. Terrific, he thought with disgust.

He went over to the closed bedroom door and knocked softly.

Then again.

And a third time.

Lord, she must sleep like a rock, Mitch thought as he gingerly opened the door.

The bed had not been slept in.

"Sasha?" A prickle of fear had the hair on the nape of his neck standing up. "Are you still in the bath?"

When he received no answer, he crossed the room in three long strides. The bathroom door was open and he was vastly relieved to see that the tub was empty. For a fleeting, terrifying moment he'd pictured her lying beneath the water, having fallen unconscious while he'd been sacked out in the living room.

"Damn!"

Frustration kept him from appreciating the fragrant pink surroundings, although the thought did cross his mind that most honeymooners sharing this suite would undoubtedly discover that the huge tub held vast erotic possibilities.

Her luggage was still in the bedroom, which Mitch took as a good sign. Unfortunately, the sight of her suit draped over the back of a pink velvet chair revealed that she'd changed her clothes. He hoped it wouldn't be necessary to give the police a description of what she was wearing.

The police? He dragged his hand through his hair and asked himself what the hell he was thinking of. Obviously, she'd simply gotten tired of waiting for him to wake up, and had gone downstairs to have lunch by herself.

The note, which he finally found in the living room propped up on the coffee table, where he'd obviously been meant to see it as soon as he woke up, said exactly that. Mitch didn't think he'd ever felt so relieved, not even when he'd escaped that burning house with a twin baby beneath each arm.

The problem was, Sasha was too damn naive. Too trusting. Hell, he could imagine her opening the door to anyone. If anything had happened to her, Mitch knew he'd have never forgiven himself. And then there was the little matter of what Glory and Jake would have done to him.

As he rode the elevator down to the first floor where the coffee shop was located just off the lobby, Mitch assured himself that the only reason he was actually looking forward to having lunch with his bride was that it had been too many hours since he'd eaten.

"Are you certain you haven't seen her?" Mitch asked the statuesque forty-something hostess who had the look of a former showgirl. "She's about this tall—" he held his hand up to his shoulder "—long, dark, wavy hair, dark brown eyes, about one-hundred-and-five pounds—"

"I told you, honey, I haven't seen her. But you're welcome to look around."

"I've looked around. Hell, I've been through this restaurant three times. And I tell you, she isn't here!"

"If you'd been paying attention, you'd realize that there aren't any women in here, period. Just a bunch of Shriners wearing hats with red tassels. These are guys who like to have a good time. And a single girl as young and good-looking as the one you've described would definitely classify as a good time. Believe me, if she had been here, everyone would have noticed."

"She's not single," he snapped without thinking. "She's married. As of two hours ago."

The woman lifted an auburn brow. "And you lost her already? That's not a real encouraging start to a marriage."

When a couple of Shriners waiting to be seated laughed at her teasing remark, Mitch began grinding his teeth. "Not that it's any of your business, but I fell asleep. When I woke up she was gone."

"Can't say as I blame her." The hostess picked up same menus. "So, you want to sit down and hope she shows up?"

The note Sasha had written said she was coming down here. But if she hadn't arrived yet, obviously something had happened to change her plans. Mitch only hoped she hadn't been waylaid by a bunch of drunk conventioneers. Although he knew their reputation for good works, Shriners were also renowned for their wild conventions.

"Where can I find the head of security?"

She shook her head. "You're overreacting, hotshot. She'll be back when she decides she's punished you enough."

"Sasha isn't the type to play those kinds of games." Even though he hardly knew her, instinct told Mitch that his bride didn't have a deceitful bone in her body.

"Every woman plays games," the hostess corrected flippantly. "It's the only way we can stay ahead of you men." With that closing remark, she led the waiting conventioneers to a table that had just been cleared.

Frustrated, Mitch left the coffee shop and was contemplating whether to check out the hotel's other restaurants first, or to go straight to security, when the sound of familiar laughter coming from the adjacent casino caught his attention.

It was there he found her, seated at a blackjack table. The combination of the tall chair and the short denim skirt she was wearing revealed a distracting bit of firm thigh.

Not surprisingly, she was surrounded by a group of boisterous males, all wearing the familiar Shriner fez. Although most of the men appeared old enough to be her father, something that felt remarkably, uncomfortably like jealousy, stirred in his gut.

"What the hell do you think you're doing?"

She looked up at him in surprise. Then smiled in a way that could have melted all the ice over the North Pole. "Hi, Mitch! Did you have a nice nap?"

Mitch wasn't in the mood for small talk. "Why aren't you in the coffee shop? Where you belong?"

"Oh." She flashed him another beneficent smile, even more dazzling than the first. Her eyes were bright and gleamed like onyx. "I was on my way there, when I noticed this room. So I came in, thinking I would watch for just a moment, when Ben gave me a dollar to play in the slot ma chine.''

''Ben?'' Dammit, it was jealousy, Mitch realized with astonishment. And it had claws.

''Ben Houston,'' a deep voice with a Texas twang boomed. A hand the size of a catcher's mitt was thrust to-ward Mitch. ''From Dallas, Texas. You must be the Mitch we've all been hearing so much about. This little girl does go on and on about you.''

''I'm Mitch Cudahy.'' Mitch's tone was hard. ''And Sasha's not a little girl. She's my wife.''

''She told us all about your wedding,'' Ben said, ignor-ing the warning edge to Mitch's voice. ''Congratulations. You've got yourself one sweet peach of a bride.''

There was a wave of enthusiastic approval from the other Shriners gathered around her chair. As he watched more than one pair of greedy male eyes practically eating Sasha up, Mitch's hands curled into fists at his side.

''I thought you were hungry.''

''Oh.'' Her eyes widened in surprise. ''I was.'' When she shrugged, the blouse slid off one shoulder revealing a creamy bit of flesh. ''But I have been having so much fun, I forgot.''

''Well, I could use something to eat.'' Mitch knew he sounded stiff, almost stodgy, and he hated himself for it. And hated her for making him feel like something he wasn't.

''Oh.'' She frowned. ''I'm sorry, Mitch. I should have thought of that.''

When the dealer cleared his throat, Sasha treated him to a smile almost as warm and wonderful as the one she'd greeted Mitch with. ''I guess I had better stop playing now.''

''You've been gambling? All this time?'' That idea had never occurred to Mitch. He'd figured she was just keeping this Houston guy company.

Mitch knew she didn't have any money of her own. Surely, he thought wildly, the house manager wouldn't have given her credit? But then again, the hotel did have his credit card number. What if she'd used it to get an advance? As his wife, she'd probably be entitled to.

"It didn't seem so very long," Sasha explained. "The time went by very fast."

Terrific. She'd undoubtedly bankrupted him. "So, how much have you lost?"

"Hell, Cudahy," Ben Houston's voice boomed again, "your little lady didn't lose. She's been beating the socks off the house for the past two hours. From the slots to roulette to blackjack."

"Ben taught me how to play blackjack." Sasha grinned up at the oilman standing beside her. "I like it very much."

"That's cause you're damn good at it, sweetheart," Ben said. He winked at Mitch. "I'll bet you didn't know you'd married a gal with a near photographic memory. If she was any better, the management would throw her out of here for card counting."

"You've been winning?"

"Yes!" She waved her hand, drawing his attention to the towering stacks of red, white and black plastic chips in front of her. It was then Mitch also noticed the half-empty champagne flute. "I have been very lucky, Mitch. Ben says I'm his good luck charm."

Mitch stared at Sasha, then down at the chips, then his eyes moved questioningly back to his bride. "How much do all those chips represent?"

"I don't know. When we left the roulette wheel I had eight thousand dollars. But we've been winning more over here, and as Ben taught me, the odds are better, so—"

"Eight thousand?" His voice cracked. "You've won eight thousand?"

"More than that," she reminded him.

"I'd say she's around twelve, give or take a few hundred," Ben offered.

"Twelve thousand dollars?"

"Not peanuts, boy," Ben said, slapping him on the back. "And although we hate like the dickens to give our little Sasha up, I suppose you'd kinda like to have her to yourself for a while." His lips curved in a masculine grin. "Considerin' that this is your honeymoon and all."

"Yes, I would definitely like some time alone with my wife." Mitch was still having trouble taking it all in. "Where did you get the money in the first place?"

"Ben gave me a dollar." She smiled up at the man, who grinned back, annoying Mitch even more. "Then I won the jackpot. And a very nice woman brought me some champagne." Her smile softened. "Have you ever had champagne, Mitch?"

"Sure."

"This was my first time." She sighed happily. "I think it is my very favorite drink." She smiled at him over the rim of the glass before polishing it off. "Can we have some more with lunch?"

"Why not," he agreed absently, his attention drawn back to that amazing stack of chips. "It appears you can afford it."

"I won them for you, Mitch," she said earnestly as she slid down from the chair. "To pay you back for the wedding and the ring, and . . ."

Before she could finish her sentence, her legs suddenly folded. If Mitch hadn't caught her, she would have fallen onto the crimson-and-gold carpeting.

"I do not understand." She gave a silvery little giggle. "My legs seem to have fallen asleep." She was holding on to him, her arms wrapped around his neck, her body against his, her breath coming in soft puffs against his throat.

For the first time Mitch realized that her words were faintly slurred. "How much of that champagne have you drunk?"

She tilted her head back and looked into his suddenly narrowed eyes, which was difficult to do the way he kept going in and out of focus. Sasha blinked to clear her vision. "I do not know, exactly." When she began to sway, his hands settled more firmly at her waist, literally holding her up. "Every time I won, the waitress brought me more." He was so fuzzy! Sasha blinked again. "Did you know that it is free?"

"So I've heard. I also know you're smashed "

"Smashed?"

"Drunk." Last year a group of Russian firemen had toured the U.S. to learn modern fire-fighting techniques. When they'd arrived in Phoenix, Mitch had been assigned to show them around. The experience, which had included visits to all of Phoenix's popular watering holes, proved helpful now as he recalled one of the few Russian words he'd learned. *"Pyahnyj."*

"Oh." She considered that for a moment as she continued to cling to him. Then she giggled. "I think, Mitch, that you are right."

Her musical laughter set the others off, as well. For his part, Mitch found little humor in the fact that his bride of two hours had gotten drunk with a bunch of Shriners in a casino.

"I'd better get you upstairs to bed."

When that suggestion earned a roar of appreciative laughter, Mitch experienced a hot urge to slam a well-placed fist into a few grinning faces. But since Sasha obviously wasn't the only one who'd had too much to drink, and the last thing he needed was to start a drunken brawl, he managed to rein in his uncharacteristic anger. "Let's get out of here."

This was easier said than done. When he released her to scoop up the chips, she began to crumble bonelessly to the floor again. Fortunately, once again, he caught her just in time.

While he tried to figure out what to do, a dark-haired man appeared at his elbow. "I'm Quenton Vaughn, manager of the casino," he told Mitch. The slim gold badge on his lapel confirmed his words. "Why don't you let me cash in your wife's winnings for you, Mr. Cudahy? And I'll have a cashier's check delivered to your suite."

"That's so wunnerfully nice of you," Sasha said before Mitch could answer. She tilted her head back, and smiled blurrily up at Mitch. "Isn't that nice, Mitch?"

"Yeah." Her arched back succeeded in pressing her hips closer against his, which did nothing to soothe his discomfort. "Real nice."

He started to sling her over his shoulder fireman style, then, remembering the brevity of her denim miniskirt, cradled her in his arms instead. He left the casino followed by waves of laughter and applause.

Although her brain was strangely fogged, it gradually occurred to Sasha that Mitch had not smiled once since he'd entered the casino.

"Mitch?"

"What?" The elevator walls were mirrored, allowing a disconcerting view of lace-trimmed panties. The skirt really was indecent, he decided.

"You are mad at me, yes?"

Sighing, he looked down into her lovely face, where a watery sheen brightened her eyes. Fearing a crying jag, he said, "I'm not mad at you, Sasha."

"But you are not happy."

"Of course I'm happy," he retorted. "Why shouldn't I be happy? I go to sleep after a hellish night trying to keep Phoenix from burning to the damn ground, then I wake up and find my bride of two hours has deserted me in order to play roulette with a bunch of drunk Shriners. And gotten smashed, besides. What man wouldn't be thrilled?"

"I did not mean to get smashed," she said earnestly. "But when I began winning—"

"You've explained all that."

His tone was sharp. And final. She fell silent and bit her lip to keep from embarrassing them both by crying again.

As the elevator continued its climb up to the tower suite, neither Mitch nor Sasha said a word.

"Mitch?" she asked as the mirrored doors finally opened on their floor.

"Yeah?"

"I did not think you would be angry." Her voice was thickening. He could hear the tears. "I left you a note."

"I wasn't angry, dammit. Not in the beginning. Not until I got scared something had happened to you."

She thought about that, struggling to clear the cobwebs from her head as he marched down the hallway. "You were worried about me?"

"Of course." He had to juggle her in his arms as he dug into his jeans for the coded card key to the room.

That was nice, Sasha decided. Surely a man would not be concerned if he didn't care, just a little.

His next words dashed her faint hope. "I'm a fireman. Worrying about people comes with the territory."

It was true. But what Mitch was not prepared to admit, even to himself, was that the cold fear he'd experienced when Sasha wasn't in the coffee shop was like none he'd ever before felt.

He carried her into the bedroom, and tossed her unceremoniously onto the bed, creating waves. "You'd better try to sleep some of that champagne off. I'll call room service."

His tone was flat and uncaring. Sasha sighed, trying to recapture a bit of the pleasure she'd experienced before Mitch's arrival in the casino.

"Mitch?"

"What now?"

Although it was difficult, she managed to push herself up to her knees, wrap her arms around his waist and press her cheek to his chest. "I am truly sorry that I upset you. Especially after you were so kind to marry me."

Hell. He reached out, intending to put his hands on her shoulders to push her away. Instead they found their way into her hair. "Sasha—"

"Please, Mitch." She held on tighter. "Do not tell me you would do it for anyone. Even if it is the truth."

The anger and frustration drained out of him and was replaced by something far more dangerous. "That wasn't what I was going to say." He buried his face in her lush, fragrant hair and felt himself slipping deeper and deeper into hot water.

They stayed that way for a long, silent time, holding on to each other. The air between them grew thick with unspoken thoughts.

She could feel his heart pounding beneath her cheek, hard and fast. Her need for him was so powerful, so staggering, that it made her tremble. Something deep and secret inside her was struggling for release. Something that could no longer be denied.

"Back in the chapel," she murmured against his chest, "before you fainted—"

"Thanks for bringing that up," he muttered.

"I was just wondering something."

"What's that?" Mitch asked distractedly. Her hair felt like silk and smelled like flowers.

"Is our marriage official? If you did not kiss me as the minister instructed?"

The dangerous words vibrated against his chest, seeping into his bloodstream. Did she know what she was doing? Did all Russian women foolishly play with fire this way? Or was Sasha Mikhailova—Sasha Cudahy, he reminded himself—unique?

When she pressed her lips against his shirt, the last of his good intentions fled. He tangled a fist in her hair and tugged, pulling her head back.

"You're right. It's high time I kissed my bride."

His mouth took hers quickly. Stunningly. She hadn't expected it to be so hot, or so hungry. Kissing Mitch was glorious. And terrifying.

"You're supposed to close your eyes," he murmured against her champagne-sweet mouth.

"If I close my eyes, I will not be able to look at you." Her fingers climbed up his neck to cup the back of his head. "I like looking at you, Mitch."

"Not as much as I like looking at you." He tilted his head, changing the angle of the kiss. "But I want to kiss you properly. So, close your eyes, sweetheart." He pressed his lips against her lids, encouraging them to flutter shut.

As his mouth took a slow, sensual journey over her face, she felt the scrape of his afternoon beard against her cheek and the pleasure of it, dark and dangerous, lanced through her.

"Lord, you are sweet." His hands pushed her blouse off her shoulders, allowing his lips access to silken perfumed flesh. "And warm."

When his hot, wicked mouth left a trail of sparks on the way back up to her tingling lips, Sasha heard a ragged sob and realized through her swimming senses that it was coming from her own burning throat.

The little sounds she was making, along with the way she was moving her lush feminine body against his, made Mitch feel about to burst. It was not something he was accustomed to feeling from a mere kiss.

To prove to himself that he'd not lost control, Mitch decided to court danger a little further.

"Open your mouth for me, sweetheart." His thumb tugged at her rosy lips. "Let me kiss you the way a woman like you should be kissed."

A woman like her. He made her sound special. Desirable. Loved. Melting against him, Sasha did as instructed, accepting his plundering tongue as she longed to accept his heart.

It was only a kiss, Mitch reminded himself. He could end it anytime. His hands roved down her body, brushing the sides of her breasts, before settling on the shapeliest little butt he'd ever felt. He pulled her tight against him, so close he could feel their hearts beating in the same wild rhythm.

He wanted her. Here. Now. He wanted to drag her down on to the wildly rocking mattress, strip off her clothes and taste every ounce of her warm flesh. He wanted to bury himself deep inside her, so deep and so hard the heat of their bodies would raise the water in the bed to boiling point.

It was when he realized that he was on the verge of doing exactly that, Mitch became vividly aware of how close he'd come to a line he dared not cross.

"Mitch?" She swayed when he abruptly released her, her hands reached for him, her eyes were wide and confused. And laced with a passion he could still taste.

"You'd better get some sleep, Sasha." She was as pale as milk. Not wanting her to fall off the bed onto her face, he took hold of her bare shoulders and lowered her gently but firmly to the mattress. "You're going to have one helluva hangover."

"I do not understand. I thought you wanted me."

Her accent had thickened. Mitch could hear the hurt in her voice. See it in her eyes. "Any man would want you, Sasha. You're beautiful and sexy as hell. But that's all it is. Animal attraction. It happens."

"Perhaps to you." The vast quantity of champagne she'd drunk allowed her to say something that under any other circumstances she would have wisely kept to herself. "But nothing even close to this has ever happened to me, Mitch." Her teeth nervously began worrying her ravished bottom lip. "No one has ever made me feel the way you do."

As he felt himself being inexorably drawn into Sasha's warm, doe-brown eyes, Mitch felt something move through him that was more complex than lust, more dangerous than desire.

"It's the champagne." Knowing it could be fatal to touch her, but unable to resist, he ran his palm down the tousled silk of her hair. "Go to sleep, Sasha. You'll feel differently after the buzz wears off."

With those less than encouraging words ringing in her ears, Mitch left the room. A moment later she heard him making a telephone call on the other side of the closed door.

Reminding herself that she was a survivor, Sasha vowed that she wasn't going to let Mitch Cudahy break her heart. If he wanted to claim that the heated kiss meant nothing to him, that was fine with her. Because she didn't care. She wouldn't let herself care.

Sasha's last thought, as she drifted off into an alcohol-induced sleep, was to wonder when she'd become such a liar.

Mitch ate a solitary dinner, and as evening gave way to night, he sprawled on the couch, staring out the undraped windows at the lights of the gambling city. And thought about Sasha, warm and oh, so very willing, just on the other side of the door.

He could have had her. And if the kisses they'd shared were any indication of the passion lurking inside her, it would have been incomparable.

But then what? Although the license on the coffee table declared them to be man and wife, they'd gone into this agreeing that it was only a marriage of convenience, designed to get immigration off her back.

If he were to make love to his bride, which he had every legal right to do, he reminded himself, he'd be taking advantage of her sweet and generous emotions. And Sasha was the kind of woman who deserved more than a passionate one-night tumble on a waterbed. She deserved a real marriage, with a husband who'd mow the lawn and take out the trash because he adored her, and a passel of gorgeous, dark-eyed kids who looked just like her.

What she deserved was the happy-ever-after ending that was a staple of Russian fairy tales. And unfortunately, since he had no intention of tying himself down to one woman for the rest of his life, he was not the man to give it to her.

That being the case, it was important that he maintain some physical—and emotional—distance.

Which was going to be a helluva lot easier said than done.

Just thinking about Sasha made his body ache in a way it hadn't since his hormone-driven teenage days. As he lay in the dark, trying to keep erotic fantasies about his bride at bay, the sounds of yet another Elvis impersonator singing drifted up from the cocktail lounge on the floor below.

When the baritone voice began singing "Are You Lonesome Tonight?" Mitch cursed.

Timing, he thought with an agonized groan, was indeed, everything.

When the garbage truck roared thropum? Ask you, says
reasing. Mitch hoped
Duning to knowing it was an organized press, which when
he'd gone

6

NEITHER MITCH nor Sasha mentioned the kiss the following morning. Nor was it brought up during the long and silent drive back to Phoenix after a new starter had been installed in the Mustang.

But they both were thinking about it. A lot.

"I'm afraid Jake was right about the place being a mess," Mitch mumbled as he carried Sasha's suitcases up the outside stairs leading to his second-story apartment. His voice sounded rusty from all the hours of disuse. He cleared his throat. "But, all this happened so quickly—"

"You don't have to apologize to me, Mitch," Sasha said quickly. Too quickly, Mitch thought, which revealed her own nervousness about the situation.

He opened the door and stared. Obviously some fairy godmother had waved her magic feather duster over the place while he'd been away getting married in Laughlin.

"It's very nice," Sasha said, her own surprise evident. It also occurred to her that if Mitch considered this Spartan example of housekeeping excellence a mess, he was going to be less than pleased with her housekeeping skills. She could literally see her reflection in the gleaming cherry end table. "And very clean."

Mitch ran his finger over the top of the television, which, when he'd gone to work four days ago, had looked as if it had been frosted with a layer of snow. "It is that," he agreed absently.

It was more than the fact that a guy could go blind from the sun streaming through the polished windows and reflecting off the shining furniture that had the apartment looking so unfamiliar. There was also the little fact that the furniture was not the same.

The cherry end table and the candlestick lamp, for example. And what the hell had happened to his couch? All right, so it might have had a few broken springs. And perhaps the stuffing was coming through the cracks in the burgundy red leather. But it had been huge. And if a guy spilled some salsa or beer on it while watching a football game on the tube, nobody cared.

Unfortunately, he could not say that for the new blue-checked cotton sofa that had taken its place. What kind of people broke into a place, took your stuff and replaced it with new?

"Oh, look," Sasha called from the adjoining kitchen, "fresh flowers!"

The minute he saw the handwriting on the white envelope stuck in the bouquet of perky yellow-faced daisies, tiger lilies, carnations and star asters, Mitch had his answer.

"They're from my mother." He skimmed the lines of familiar handwriting. "She wants to welcome us home."

The congratulatory note had him wondering what, exactly, Jake had revealed about the hastily planned wedding. It also explained the furniture, which, now that he thought about it, Mitch realized belonged to his grandmother Cudahy. His mother had stashed it away in her basement when his grandmother had moved into that condo on the San Diego coast.

"There's a casserole in the refrigerator we can heat up in the microwave," he continued reading. "And a bottle of champagne in the refrigerator, if you'd like a glass."

Sasha put her hand to her head, which, while not throbbing as badly as it had when she woke up this morning, still felt as if someone had hit her with a very sharp rock. "I think I've had enough champagne for one weekend."

"Hangovers are the pits."

He'd watched her obvious suffering all day and although he'd experienced random urges to offer her sympathy and aspirin, he'd resisted both. There was something about Sasha that encouraged a man to want to protect her, to take care of her. And, dammit, to care for her.

And that definitely wasn't the plan, he reminded himself as a ball of ice formed in his stomach.

Get married, get that bureaucratic weasel Potter off her back, help her get a green card and move on. That was the plan. And so long as they both stuck to it, everything would be okay.

She looked at him with interest. "You have felt this way?"

He laughed. "Sweetheart, more times than I care to count."

There it was again, that easy endearment that made her heart turn somersaults. Sasha reminded herself that the only reason she was standing here, in Mitch's spotless sun-warmed kitchen that smelled of lemon cleanser and spring flowers was to trick the U.S. government.

Mitch had been chivalrous enough to come up with the marriage ruse in the first place. It was not his fault she loved him. It was not his fault that she'd lain awake last night, fantasizing about a real wedding night.

If her heart was suffering, the pain, like her pounding headache, would pass. And in the meantime, she'd just have to keep reminding herself that thinking too much about Mitch—especially thinking about tomorrows with Mitch—would be a very grave mistake.

They stood there, on either side of the kitchen table, the wicker basket of flowers between them, looking at each other, attempting to hide their feelings.

As he felt himself being pulled into the velvety warmth of her eyes, the icy knot in his stomach pulled even tighter and Mitch realized that if he didn't get out of here now, he'd be in danger of suffocating.

"Why don't you unpack?" he suggested, waving his hand in the general vicinity of the single bedroom. "I've got some errands to run."

It was more than a little obvious that he was desperate to escape. Sasha lowered her eyes and began toying nervously with the flowers, rubbing the ruffled edges of a white carnation between her thumb and index finger. "Will you be back for dinner?" The words were no sooner out of her mouth than she wished she could retrieve them.

Hell, she was already starting to sound like a wife. That's all he needed. Deciding to establish the parameters of this mock marriage now, before things got entirely out of hand, Mitch shrugged. "I don't know. But it'd probably be better if you didn't wait for me."

His voice was more distant than she'd ever heard it. Deciding she liked him better when he was yelling at her, and refusing to allow him to see that his cold dismissal stung so cruelly, she lifted her chin and gave him a look of icy aloofness that one of her czarist ancestors might have used to demoralize a recalcitrant servant.

"Fine. I am accustomed to eating alone. And I was not attempting to control your behavior."

"Good. Because, just for the record, others have tried. But no one has succeeded."

Now they were even sniping at each other like an old married couple. Deciding that this must've been the shortest honeymoon on record, Mitch clenched his teeth and met her cool, level gaze. "Use whatever drawers and closet space you need."

With that he was gone. Almost, but not quite, slamming the door behind him.

Sasha sank down onto one of the Windsor kitchen chairs and sighed. But having already cried more in the last few days than she had in her entire twenty-four years, her eyes remained resolutely dry.

"DARLING!" Meredith smiled in welcome when she opened the door to her townhouse and saw him standing on her front porch. "I didn't expect you."

"We need to talk."

"This sounds serious."

"Not really. Well, I guess it is, in a way." Mitch dragged his hand through his hair. "Can I just come in, so we don't have to have this conversation in front of an audience?"

Meredith glanced past him toward the elderly woman walking the ancient Schnauzer, as she did each afternoon, rain or shine. "Of course." She moved aside to let him in, and waved to her neighbor.

"Good evening, Mrs. Lansky," she called out in those perfectly modulated tones that always reminded critics of Diane Sawyer. "How is Petey tonight?"

"His arthritis seems to be easing up," the elderly woman answered. "In fact, he hasn't had so much spring in his step since he was a pup. I think it's the new dog food I switched him to after your consumer report last month."

"I'm glad to hear that." Meredith's smile could have melted butter. "I have a life-style segment tonight that might interest you—it's about a gourmet restaurant catering to dogs.''

"That does sound interesting.'' The elderly woman nodded her snowy head. "Petey and I never miss a broadcast.'' That said, owner and dog continued down the walk.

"Stroking your public again?'' Mitch asked as he threw himself down on the white silk sofa. The first time he'd entered Meredith's house, he'd felt as if he'd stumbled into a blizzard. Or a hospital emergency room. Everything—floor, walls, furniture, silk flowers—was as white as snow.

"Laugh all you want to, Mitch, darling. But my Q-ratings are the highest in the Rocky Mountain region.''

"I always thought that was because of your legs.'' Despite the seriousness of his mission, his gaze drifted down to the long legs attractively showcased by the short emerald silk robe.

"Anyone ever tell you that you're a terrible chauvinist, Cudahy?''

"All the time.'' In spite of the seriousness of his mission, he grinned. "Personally, I've always taken it as a badge of honor.''

"You would.'' She sighed dramatically. "Although I have to admit that if there's one man who can get away with it, it may be you.'' She leaned down and planted a kiss on his mouth. It was hot and long and involved a lot of the clever tongue action she did so well. "I missed you the other night,'' she said when the kiss ended.

"I was out of town.''

"That's what Jake told me when I called the station. So, does this sudden need to get away have anything to do with your reason for coming here?''

"What makes you think that?''

"From your grim expression, darling, I have the impression that you haven't dropped in for a quickie before I leave for the 6:00 p.m. newscast."

"No."

"I didn't think so." She sighed and glanced down at her watch. "We don't have a lot of time. Why don't you come talk to me while I redo my makeup?"

He followed her into the bedroom, which, like the living room, was a sea of white, suggesting the same Grace Kelly restraint she wore like a second skin in public. Having discovered firsthand exactly how unrestrained the newscaster could be while tumbling around in those white satin sheets, Mitch knew the cool outward appearance was deceiving.

Which was, he reminded himself, what his wedding to Sasha was all about. Deception.

"I don't want you to start throwing things," he warned as he watched her smooth moisturizer into her skin with her fingertips, "until you hear the entire story."

"Gracious." She met his eyes in her mirror. "This does sound serious."

At least he had her full attention. Sometime between explaining who exactly Sasha Mikhailova was, and ending with yesterday's wedding ceremony—leaving out the fact that he'd fainted and the part about Elvis and Sasha's incredible streak of luck at the tables—Mitch was aware of Meredith abandoning her tubes and pots.

"Well," she said when he finally finished, "that's quite a story." She turned around on the little white satin stool and began sponging on her foundation.

Mitch warily watched her, waiting for the explosion he figured would eventually come. The silence was beginning to drive him crazy.

"Since the wedding wasn't real, there really isn't any reason for us to stop seeing one another," he said reassuringly.

"Don't you mean sleeping together?" she asked, moving on to rose-tinted blusher.

"Well, yeah." He knew he was mumbling and hated himself for it. "I guess that's what I mean."

She accented her eyes with a smudge of kohl at the corners, and applied three coats of mascara. "May I ask a few questions?" she asked finally, after outlining her lips with a vermillion pencil.

"I'd say you're entitled, given the circumstances."

"Did you happen to tell your new bride you were coming here?"

"Not exactly."

"Why not? If this is simply a marriage of convenience, why should she care what you do? Or with whom you do it?"

"It's more complicated than that."

"Most marriages are," Meredith said sagely. Since she'd already made three trips to the altar before the age of twenty-eight, Mitch figured she knew more about such things than he did.

"But it's still just a green card marriage," he insisted.

"So you said." She filled in the vermillion line with a bright crimson, pressed her lips against a tissue, then turned to face him.

Here we go, thought Mitch as he steeled himself for the fireworks.

"But I don't have time to get sidetracked with personal discussions right now," Meredith said calmly, "not when we have something far more important to discuss."

Mitch, who'd been balanced on the balls of his feet prepared to duck flying tubes, jars and bottles, released his guard somewhat. But Meredith's next statement had the effect of a fist to his midriff, leaving him breathless.

"Mitch," she said sweetly, "I want you to get me an exclusive interview with your bride."

"I DON'T GET THIS," Jake said as he dribbled the basketball. "Are you telling me that you're ticked off because your lover isn't mad at you for getting married?"

"The least Meredith could've done was act a little put out," Mitch complained, anticipating Jake's move to the right. After leaving Meredith's, he'd dropped by the station, hoping to find his brother-in-law working out on the court. They'd been playing one-on-one for the past half hour, he was having the damn pants beat off him, and after thirty minutes of sweating and running, he was still as frustrated as he'd been when he'd arrived. "And it isn't a real marriage." He switched to the left.

"Who are you trying to convince? Me? Or yourself?" Jake feigned right, moved left, and sank a nice easy jump shot. "He shoots. He scores! And the crowd goes wild."

"You traveled," Mitch complained as he took Jake's pass and began dribbling the ball. "And you also sound just like Meredith."

"She didn't buy the marriage-of-convenience story, either?"

"No." Mitch swore as Jake deftly stole the ball and shot another quick two points from the perimeter. "How the hell do you expect me to concentrate on my game when you keep bringing up my damn marriage?"

Jake tossed him another pass. "Sorry. I thought you came here to talk."

"Well, you're wrong." Mitch cursed again as he threw up a brick that missed the rim by a mile. The ball went rolling off the court, and came to a stop against the wheel of a fire truck. "I came here because I don't have anywhere else to go."

Jake eyed the ball and shrugged, deciding to let it go, for now. "How about home?"

"Which home? The comfortable, messy one I used to live in? The one with the leather couch? The one that didn't smell like a lemon orchard and look like an explosion at a rose parade?"

"Ah." Jake nodded sagely. "I told Katie I thought that was a mistake."

"Obviously she didn't listen," Mitch muttered.

"When you've been married a bit longer, you'll realize that women never listen when it comes to decorating or matchmaking."

"I don't intend to be married all that much longer. And I want my couch back." Mitch raked his hand through his hair and glared at the late rush-hour traffic streaming by the station. "Hell, I want my life back."

"Let me see if I've got this right. You're ticked off at your mom and Katie for getting rid of your couch, so you're going to take it out on Sasha by leaving her alone her first night as a married woman."

"It's not her first night."

"That's right." Jake leaned against the backboard post, folded his arms across his broad chest and eyed Mitch with amusement. "You two had an unexpected honeymoon in Laughlin. So, how did it go?"

"It didn't." Although he didn't elaborate, Mitch's scowl spoke volumes.

"Sounds as if you wish otherwise."

"And you sound like some damn radio talk show shrink!" Mitch's outburst caused a trio of pigeons perched on the roof to flap their wings and fly off to the top of a nearby palm tree.

"You probably just need to get laid," Jake said, laughing. "Which, I figure, probably makes sense. I doubt if there are many guys who could spend the night with Sasha and not want to jump her lush little Russian bones.''

Mitch's hands curled unconsciously into fists at his side. "Keep that up and I'll have to kill you."

Humor was mixed with the open speculation in Jake's gaze. "Now you sound like a husband."

Mitch's muttered curse was ripe and vulgar. "It's just that she's a nice woman."

"The best," Jake agreed. "And the little fact that she's in love with you probably makes this marriage thing stickier."

"She's not in love with me," Mitch snapped. The idea was as ridiculous as it was horrifying.

"She's been bonkers over you since you showed up at the diner like Sir Galahad in a yellow coat and helmet." The laughter left his eyes as his gaze turned serious. "Which is why you're going to have to tread carefully, pal. Because if you break that little girl's heart, there'll be a whole bunch of people standing in line waiting to kick out your lung."

"Beginning with you?"

"Nah." Jake shook his head as his natural humor returned. "Glory will be first. But I'll be right behind her. Followed, I'll bet, by your mom and sister." He nodded in the direction of the station house. "Then the rest of the crew. Then Glory's regular customers, then—"

"I get the idea." Mitch's shoulders drooped as he realized exactly how deep a mess he'd gotten himself into this time. Compared to this phony marriage gambit, rushing into blazing buildings seemed like a lead pipe cinch.

"You want to play some more?" Jake asked. "Or go get drunk?"

"You'll just keep beating me if we play," Mitch grumbled. "So I guess the only thing left to do is get drunk."

"You could go home."

"No." Mitch shook his head. "That's not an option."

It was Jake's turn to curse as he shook his head. "I'll drive. Just let me call Katie." A smile twitched. "Some of us have learned the wisdom of letting the little woman know we'll be late."

As Jake went into the station to make his call, Mitch's mind wandered to Sasha, alone in his apartment, eating her solitary dinner. Sympathy stirred, guilt clawed treacherously at his gut.

"Ready?" Jake asked when he returned.

Reminding himself that Sasha was a big girl and had understood the rules going into this fake marriage, Mitch forced down the sympathy and tried to ignore the guilt.

"Ready." He climbed into the passenger seat of the new minivan Jake had traded his Corvette in for when the baby had been born, and told himself that this married man's car was just one more reason he had every intention of regaining his single status as soon as possible.

Marriage meant sedate wheels and exchanging Saturday night poker games with the guys for driving the baby-sitter home after an early movie. Marriage meant spending Sundays mowing lawns instead of playing softball and watching ESPN until your eyes glazed over.

Marriage meant doing dishes and changing diapers, buying life insurance, worrying about orthodontists' bills and college tuition and pretending to be interested by paint and fabric swatches.

Marriage was okay, Mitch supposed, for guys like Jake. Guys who actually seemed to enjoy their tranquil, predictable lives of suffocating domesticity.

And although Mitch was truly glad his sister had found such a paragon of a husband, he vowed that there was no way he was going to spend the rest of his life in captivity.

7

IT WAS TWO in the morning when Mitch poured himself out of the minivan and managed to stagger up the stairs. His head was swimming with a combination of Mexican beer and tequila chasers and he knew he was going to hate himself in the morning. But right now, he felt just fine.

It took him three tries before he managed to unlock the door. Then, leaving a trail of clothes across the living room carpet, he managed to make his way into the bedroom, where he threw himself facedown onto the bed, pinning Sasha with an arm thrown across her chest. And then he began to snore. Loudly.

His breath was like a warm breeze in Sasha's ear—a beer-scented breeze. When she tried to shift away, he mumbled and pulled her closer. As he held her against his chest, Sasha realized he wasn't wearing a stitch of clothing. His body was hard and warm. And undeniably inviting.

Assuring herself that she was only worried about waking him if she tried to pull away, she decided to stay right where she was. As she finally drifted off to sleep, Sasha was smiling.

Mitch dreamed he was in the islands, making love to a beautiful woman on a sun-drenched, deserted beach. Somewhere in the distance, a deep voice was crooning "Blue Hawaii." The woman fit against him perfectly. Her smooth, oiled skin carried the scent of tropical flowers. As he covered her mouth with his, her lips trembled apart on a sigh as soft as the island tradewinds. She was every bit as delicious as he'd known she would be. Her mouth tasted like ripe fruit. Kissing her was like dining on paradise.

Wanting more, he ran his hands down her body, stroking her smooth curves and taut muscles with a smooth, practiced touch that quickened her breath and drew low murmurs from between her succulent lips that in turn set off a series of fiery eruptions deep inside Mitch. He slid his knee between her thighs and dragged his mouth down her throat to her breast.

Caught up in the wonder and heat of her own erotic dream, Sasha combed her hands through Mitch's hair and murmured her pleasure in her native Russian.

The unfamiliar words had the effect of a bucket of icy water. Mitch froze, then slowly, gingerly, opened his eyes.

The bedroom was draped in deep purple shadows. But it was not so dark that Mitch couldn't see the awareness slowly flooding into Sasha's sleepy eyes.

"Aw, hell." He withdrew his hand from beneath her white cotton nightgown. "I can't believe . . . I never . . ."

With a muffled sound that was part moan and part curse, he rolled onto his back and covered his eyes with his forearm. "I didn't know," he said, his husky voice strained. "Why the hell didn't you stop me?"

"You were not the only one who was sleeping."

He took his arm away, his expression anything but encouraging. "You weren't awake?"

She gnawed a bit on her lower lip, trying to decide how much to tell him. It was true that she'd been asleep when she'd first felt his lips brush her temple. But by the time his wicked, wonderful hands had begun moving over her body, seeking out pleasure points she'd never even known she possessed, Sasha had been fully, blissfully awake.

In the end, she opted for a half-truth. "I was dreaming."

She looked so lovely, with the rosy hue of passion still blooming in her cheeks. Her eyes held a lingering vestige of desire and passion that he found almost impossible to resist. If she were any other woman, Mitch knew, now that they were both awake, they wouldn't be wasting time talking.

"That must have been some dream."

"It was quite pleasant." She tugged the rumpled sheet up nearly to her chin. "As yours must have been, as well."

Mitch felt a twinge of disappointment when she covered up those wondrous breasts that were enticingly visible beneath the thin white cotton, but reluctantly decided it was the prudent thing to do.

"I haven't woken up so horny since I was seventeen."

The word was unfamiliar. But Sasha did not need a Russian/English dictionary to understand its meaning. "I have never before woken up feeling like that," she admitted.

He'd suspected as much. "I should have sacked out on the couch. But by the time I crawled home, I'd forgotten you'd be here."

Although she knew he hadn't meant the words as an insult, they stung nonetheless. "I should not have taken your bed."

"Don't be silly. You're a guest. You get the bed."

"But—"

"I said, you get the damn bed." Frustration sharpened his tone. "Don't argue with me on this one, Sasha. Not while a sadistic maniac is pounding away inside my head with a jackhammer."

She knew the feeling. Intimately. "You have a hangover?"

"Not a hangover," he corrected, groaning as he sat up. "The grandpappy of all hangovers." He blinked his eyes and wondered if someone had glued sandpaper to the insides of his lids after he'd passed out. It was just the kind of sick practical joke Jake would have enjoyed.

"I'm sorry."

"It's not your fault. You didn't pour those tequila chasers down my throat."

"No. But if you hadn't been trying to stay away from me, you would have come home earlier."

He opened his mouth to lie and knew he wouldn't be able to pull it off. What she'd said was the truth. And they both knew it.

"I'd better brush my teeth." He pushed aside the sheet on his side of the double bed. "I think a badger must've died in my mouth while I was sleeping."

She watched him walk into the bathroom with the casual air of a man comfortable with nudity. Which, she considered, made sense. What man wouldn't enjoy showing off such a perfect body?

She heard the sound of water running, and the flush of the toilet. And then she heard him turn on the shower. When her unruly mind pictured Mitch standing beneath the stream of hot water, she closed her eyes, tight, trying to block the provocative image. But it didn't work.

It was still with her, lingering in her mind as she dressed for their meeting with Mr. Donald O. Potter.

Sasha had never seen Mitch in a suit. As she entered the kitchen after her own shower, she thought he looked even more handsome than he did in his usual polo shirt and jeans. And the blue tie exactly matched his eyes.

She stifled a sigh, wishing he really was her husband.

"You look very nice," she murmured as she took out a carton of orange juice out of the fridge.

"I feel like a man on the verge of death." He took the carton from her and poured the juice. The way her hands were shaking, he was afraid she'd pour it all over the counter, herself and the tile floor his mother and sister had gleaming with a mirrorlike sheen.

He took a look at her unadorned white blouse, navy skirt and flats. Although the plain-Jane clothes weren't any more appealing than the suit she'd worn for their wedding, he decided that Sasha was a woman who would probably look gorgeous in a gunny sack.

"You look pretty." It was the truth. "But a little pale." That, too, was the truth. His eyes narrowed as they moved over her face. "Wait here."

He left the room and returned with a tube of cream blush. He unscrewed the cap, squeezed a dot onto the end of his finger, then smoothed the soft rose cream along the slanted line of first one cheekbone, then the other. His fingers created an enervating warmth that nearly made her knees buckle.

He stepped back to study the results. "That's better."

"You have many talents," she murmured, wondering how he'd acquired such cosmetic skills.

Mitch shrugged. "I grew up sharing a bathroom with my sister." He saw no point in revealing that years spent watching other women playing with their pots and brushes had taught him a lot. "A guy's bound to pick up a few things." He glanced at his watch, then gulped down the mug of cooling coffee he'd left on the counter. "Well, I guess it's time to face the inquisition."

The chill started at the top of her head and worked its way downward. Watching the renewed color leave her face, Mitch felt a stir of pity. She was trembling like a willow in a hurricane. Touching her was asking for trouble, he looped his arms around her waist and pressed his lips against her hair. There was no passion in either his embrace or his light kiss, only tenderness.

"It's going to be all right."

She closed her eyes and allowed herself to draw from his strength. When she felt she wouldn't humiliate herself by weeping, she tilted her head back and looked up at him.

"What if it isn't?" she asked in a soft, fractured voice that once again pulled at something elemental inside him. "What if Mr. Donald O. Potter gets his way? And I'm deported?"

"That won't happen."

"How can you be so sure?"

"Because any immigration bureaucrat who even tries to deport you is going to have to go through me, first."

He winked. "Come on, sweetheart. Let's go break the happy news of your marriage to the weasel. Then we can deposit that cashier's check from the casino in your bank account."

Sasha reminded herself that this was America, the land of promise and limitless possibilities. As she left the apartment with her new husband, she felt almost confident.

Unfortunately, that feeling was not to last long.

Sasha was not surprised when they were kept waiting. This was, after all, standard operating procedure for her nemesis. Mitch, however, did not bother to conceal his growing impatience.

"I don't get it," he growled as they waited on the hard plastic chairs in the overcrowded waiting room. "Our appointment was two hours ago. We haven't seen anyone else go in there. So what the hell is the guy doing? Pulling wings off flies?"

"He is a government employee," Sasha explained for the umpteenth time. Having experienced a lifetime of Russian bureaucratic red tape, she was more able to take the immigration officer's stalling tactics in stride.

"So am I," Mitch noted pointedly as he popped two more aspirin into his mouth and swallowed them dry. "But I wonder how Potter would like it if his damn house caught fire and I showed up two hours late to put it out."

"That is different."

"It shouldn't be."

She thought about that. "I suppose you're right. But it doesn't change things." All too aware of the aggravation surrounding Mitch like a red-hot aura, she said, "You won't say anything that will make him angry?"

"Nah." Her relief was short-lived. "I think I'll just punch his lights out."

"Mitch!"

The absolute terror in her wide eyes could not be feigned. Realizing how seriously she was taking this, Mitch instantly regretted his flippant tone.

"Sasha. Sweetheart. I was just joking." He patted her hand just as the office door opened.

"Mr. Potter can see you now, Ms. Mikhailova," the secretary, clad in a severely cut gray suit that did nothing for her scrawny figure, announced. Her expression, beneath the sixties beehive was grim.

"It's about time. And the name is Mrs. Cudahy," he said as they walked past the woman. "You might want to make a note of that in your records."

It was not, Mitch discovered, going to be easy. Although he'd not doubted Glory's statement about immigration cracking down on arranged marriages, neither had he expected to be treated like Public Enemy Number One.

From the moment he learned of their hasty marriage, Potter didn't mince words. "If you think this is going to forestall deportation proceedings against you, Ms. Mikhailova—"

"Cudahy," Mitch broke in.

"Excuse me?"

"Sasha's name is Mrs. Cudahy now."

"Yes." He pinched his thin lips together, making them practically disappear. "The timing of the marriage is quite convenient. Considering that Ms. Mik—"

"Cudahy," Mitch reminded him.

Potter gave him a long look, then shrugged, as if deciding he could afford to concede this point. After all, he had the power of the United States government behind him. What chance did these two have?

"It strikes me as very suspicious," he continued stiffly, "that Mrs. Cudahy—" he glanced at Mitch, who nodded his satisfaction "—did not mention your engagement at Friday's appointment."

"That's simple." Mitch took Sasha's cold hand in his, lacing their fingers together in an easy, familiar husbandly gesture. "She didn't know I was going to propose."

"Do you really expect me to believe that you coincidentally popped the question at the same time the government was preparing to deport your wife, Mr. Cudahy?"

Although Mitch had been insisting to everyone—including himself—that this was not a real marriage, the way the squinty-eyed little weasel had heaped an extra helping of scorn on the word "wife" made his temper flare.

Reminding himself that leaning over the spotless metal desk and planting his fist in the jerk's supercilious face would not help Sasha's cause, he reined in his anger.

"I'm not going to lie to you," he said, deciding to go with a half-truth. "Sasha's meeting with you did have something to do with my asking her to marry me." When Sasha's hand turned even icier, he squeezed it reassuringly.

"Aha!" Potter looked as if he'd just won the lottery. Once again Mitch was tempted to punch him. Once again he managed, just barely, to resist.

"It was when I realized that I could actually lose her—" he gave Sasha a fond, loving look "—that I realized I loved her. And wanted us to spend the rest of our lives together."

"That's a lovely story, Mr. Cudahy. Unfortunately, it's not the least bit original." Potter took an ominous stack of forms from the filing cabinet behind the desk. "In light of your new status, I'll need to interview you separately."

"What kind of interview?" Mitch asked. He'd figured that he'd put on the blue suit he'd bought to wear to his sister's wedding, go downtown with Sasha, explain he was her husband and walk out with her new green card in hand. An interview with the weasel hadn't been in the plan.

"For starters, we need to ensure that you're actually living together."

"Of course we are. We're married."

"Yes. So you say." Skepticism dripped from the acid tone. "Well, your wife will have to wait in the outer office. I'll question you first. Then it will be Mrs. Cudahy's turn."

Listening to the thick disbelief in the man's voice, Mitch thought that he should have just knocked the guy through his office window while he'd had the chance.

As Sasha prepared to leave the room, her lovely face more miserable than he'd ever seen it, Mitch took her chin between his fingers. "It's going to be okay," he assured her quietly. Then he captured her lips in a quick kiss.

"Sorry about that," he told a frowning Potter, "I couldn't help myself. You know how newlyweds are." With a rakish wink, he walked Sasha the few feet to the closed door, then gave her a proprietary, husbandly pat on the rear.

Sasha's head was still reeling as she sank down onto one of the chairs in the waiting room. A baby being bounced on the lap of a woman next to her screamed its discontent and nearby a husband and wife squabbled loudly. But still stunned by Mitch's hot kiss, Sasha didn't notice them.

When it was finally her turn, Sasha tried her best to answer the questions, but there were so many, and they were so intimate! Thanks to her conversations with Jake, she managed to correctly name Mitch's mother and sister and new baby niece. And from his dinner orders for the firehouse, she knew he preferred ribs over chicken, and steak to everything else. He didn't like apple pie, but warm cherry pie topped with vanilla ice cream was his favorite dessert.

These things she knew. Almost everything else—including his favorite television programs and the last book he'd read—drew a blank.

"Why don't you go on down and wait for me in the car, sweetheart?" Mitch suggested when she was finally allowed to escape the inquisition. She was as pale as a wraith. "I have something I need to do. It won't take long."

There was something in his tone, something unsettling. A dark and dangerous edge she'd never heard before. Quite honestly, it frightened her.

"Mitch?"

He ran his hand down her hair. "Don't you worry that pretty little head about a thing," he said loud enough for the avidly watching secretary to hear. "Everything's going to be okay."

Sasha, too, was aware of the secretary's interest. Not wanting to do anything that might get reported back to her enemy, she sighed, nodded, then left the office.

Mitch waited until he heard the ding of the elevator door opening. Then he marched back into Potter's office.

The immigration officer was making notations in a manila file even thicker than Sasha's. From the satisfied smirk on his face, Mitch decided the bastard must be ruining someone else's life.

He glanced up and frowned at Mitch. "I believe our interview was over, Mr. Cudahy."

"That's what you think." Mitch put both hands on the black metal desk and glared down at the man, mayhem threatening in his stance and his eyes. "I want you to listen to me, Potter. And I want you to listen good."

"What you want is none of my concern."

"Now that's where you're wrong."

Potter took one look at the thundercloud on Mitch's face and reached for the phone. "I'm going to call security."

Mitch snatched the receiver out of the man's hand. "If you don't want to end up picking your teeth off the floor, I'd suggest you listen to what I have to say."

"Are you threatening me?"

"You bet your wingtips I am." Mitch hung up the phone. "The same way you threatened my wife."

"That Russian émigré is not your wife."

"Now there you go," Mitch said with an exaggerated sigh, "questioning my veracity again. I don't really give a flying fig what you think, Potter, because I happen to have a piece of paper stating that according to the laws of Nevada—and the United States of America—Sasha is my lawfully wedded wife. My spouse. My woman. And call me oversensitive, but I don't like autocratic little jerks who make my woman cry." His fingers curled around the wrinkled brown tie as he pulled Potter toward him across the top of the desk. "If you ever so much as look crossways at Sasha again, you'll have to answer to me. And believe me, it won't be an enjoyable experience."

Potter's Adam's apple bobbed as he swallowed. "It's against the law to threaten a federal government official," he said, his attempt at bluster belied by the sickly ash color of his face.

"It'll be your word against mine," Mitch reminded him. "And who do you think the cops will believe? A squinty-eyed little weasel with yesterday's lunch on his tie? Or a genuine American hero?''

He released the tie and Potter fell back into his chair with a force that sent it rolling dangerously toward the window. Mitch was vaguely disappointed when it stopped a few inches away.

He left the office, pausing in the doorway. ''Leave my wife alone.''

As he took the elevator downstairs, Mitch was smiling.

Unfortunately his feeling of goodwill was short-lived. As he left the office building, he saw Sasha, not waiting in the car as he'd instructed, but standing on the sidewalk gazing into the window of the jewelry store next door.

At that same instant, a kid with baggy shorts, a purple and orange Phoenix Suns T-shirt and high-top sneakers grabbed her purse and took off running.

8

SASHA COULDN'T BELIEVE what was happening!

One minute she was soothing her jangled nerves by drinking in the lovely sight of diamonds and rubies in the jewelry store window. Then, in less time that it took to blink, her purse—with her valuable gambling winnings inside—had been ripped from her shoulder.

She cried out in dismay.

At the same time, she saw Mitch sprinting off after the thief.

The part of her that was desperate for the money that would help her find her father was immensely relieved that Mitch had appeared on the scene. Another, stronger part, feared he could get hurt.

Refusing to let him risk his life alone, she began running.

Mitch was proud of the way he'd kept himself fit. His work, after all, depended on his being in shape. He damned his suit and dress shoes, but vowed that there was no way this punk was going to get away with the crime.

The kid ran across the street, dodging between a city bus and a delivery truck. On his heels Mitch followed, ignoring the strident angry blast of the truck horn.

An elderly woman with pewter curls came out of a coffee shop. The thief pushed her aside, almost knocking her down, and kept running. Cursing, Mitch slowed to ensure that she was all right. He picked up her red pocketbook, handed it back to her, then rushed on.

Neither of them noticed Sasha, half a block behind, struggling to keep up.

Adrenaline was racing through Mitch's veins, pounding in his ears like the beat of a drum. He could hear his own labored breathing, feel the burning in his lungs.

The signal at the intersection said Don't Walk. The thief ignored it, shoved aside a city maintenance crew barricade, leapt over an open manhole and raced into traffic. Brakes squealed as Mitch followed.

By the time they cut across the basketball arena's outdoor courtyard, Mitch had gained on the thief. The kid might be younger, but as Mitch forced his legs to keep up their pistonlike motion, he reminded himself that he was a hero, dammit. Savior of women and children and kittens.

There was no way he was going to allow himself to be a failure in Sasha's eyes.

Even if he had to take on the entire immigration service.

Even if this ridiculous race gave him a frigging heart attack.

A bicyclist shot out of an alley between them. The purse snatcher put on an extra burst of speed just as Mitch slammed headlong into the bike, sending himself and the rider sprawling into the gutter.

His knee hit the ground with a painful cracking sound, then he skidded across the pavement, picking up gravel, making his palms feel as if they were suddenly on fire.

"Hey, man," the bicyclist complained, struggling to his feet, helmet askew, "what the hell do you think you're doing?"

"Sorry." Ignoring his aching knee and burning hands, Mitch pushed himself to his feet and took off running again.

Sasha, who'd waited impatiently at the red pedestrian signal was horrified when she saw Mitch crash into the bicycle. Her cry of alarm drew the attention of a passing motorcycle cop, who immediately pulled over to the curb.

"Something wrong, ma'am?"

"My husband!" She pointed toward Mitch. "He's trying to catch the thief who stole my handbag!"

The cop took one look at the situation, hit his siren and lights, gunned the motorcycle and took off, leaving her to watch helplessly as Mitch chased the teenager across the Civic Center plaza. Just as he reached out again, the kid put on another burst of speed.

"Dammit! That's enough!" With a low flying tackle, Mitch managed to pull the purse snatcher down.

Sasha's heart caught in her throat as she watched Mitch become airborne. He and the thief careened into the fountain and began splashing around, throwing punches while water poured down on them as if from a cloudburst.

Seconds later, the cop caught up with them.

By the time Sasha arrived on the scene, the perpetrator had been handed over to the cop. Mitch was bent over, his hands on his knees, his breathing labored. He was also soaked to the skin.

"Mitch!" She flung herself at him, almost knocking them both over in her enthusiasm. "Are you all right?"

He caught her around the waist, steadying her as he steadied himself. "I'm...fine." He dragged in a huge draft of air as he handed her the purse. "I saved...your money."

"The money is not important. Not compared to you!" She'd never made a more truthful statement. "When I saw you fall..."

"It wasn't anything." He drew in another breath that didn't hurt nearly as badly, making him think he might live, after all.

"You could have been hurt," she scolded. Now that she was no longer terrified, Sasha was angry. "Such reckless, dangerous behavior should be left to the police."

After what he'd just been through for her, Sasha's criticism stung. "In case you didn't notice, sweetheart, there weren't any police around when you decided to go window shopping with every cent to your name in your purse so every gangbanger and crook in the city could steal it!"

"I was waiting for you!"

"I told you to wait in the damn car," Mitch shouted. He dragged his hand through his wet hair in frustration and cursed the flaw that had made him chase the kid in the first place. It wasn't his job. The cops didn't fight fires—so why should he fight crime?

"Oh, Mitch!" Sasha's temper deflated like air leaving a balloon as she observed the blood smear on his temple. "You have hurt yourself." She grabbed hold of his hand and turned it over, gasping as she viewed the asphalt imbedded in his skin.

"I told you, it's nothing. A little soap and water and I'll be fine."

"Excuse me, ma'am." A third voice entered the conversation.

Sasha turned toward the motorcycle officer. The thief, she noticed, was now in the custody of a second policeman who'd been cruising by in his patrol car.

"I assume you and your husband want to press charges."

"Yes," Mitch said.

"No," Sasha said at the same time.

"What?" Mitch stared at her, unable to believe what he was hearing. "After I nearly break my neck—"

"You said it was only a little fall," she reminded him.

"After I nearly break my neck," he repeated from between clenched teeth, "chasing the little creep, what do you mean, you're not going to press charges?"

"It's not necessary," she insisted.

"The hell it isn't." He turned to the cop who was looking bored, as if he'd heard all this before. "If she doesn't want to file a complaint, I will."

"Mitch!" Sasha frowned at him, then forced a shaky smile at the policeman. "Will you excuse us, please? I would like to speak with my husband."

The cop shrugged as he pulled his leather gloves back on. "Make it quick. We can't stand around here all day."

Mitch took her arm and pulled her a few feet away. "Okay. Shoot."

"Shoot?" She glanced nervously back at the 9 mm pistol the patrolman was wearing.

"Talk to me."

"Oh." Relieved, she said, "If we press charges, we'll have to go to the police station. And sign papers, yes?"

"Sure." It was Mitch's turn to shrug. "So?"

"So, then I'll have a police file. And I'll be automatically deported."

Comprehension flickered. "Sasha, you won't have a record, the kid will. Hell, he probably already does. You'll be doing society a favor if you get him put away. Or would you rather have him steal someone else's purse? Like that little old lady he nearly knocked down?"

She knew he was right. But still . . .

"In Russia, having the police know your name is not such a good thing," she argued weakly.

With that single statement, she made all the news reports and magazine articles he'd read about life behind the former Iron Curtain come crashing home.

She looked so serious, so distressed, Mitch had a sudden urge to take her in his arms and kiss that worried frown off her face. Instead he reached out and touched her cheek with a roughened fingertip.

"This isn't Russia, sweetheart. In America you're considered a good citizen for reporting a crime."

"I have seen such things on 'Crime Stoppers,'" she admitted hesitantly. "And 'America's Most Wanted,' but—"

"But nothing. We'll go to the station, press charges, then take your money to the bank. Before anything else happens."

He could practically see the wheels turning in her head as she looked over at the waiting patrolman. "I suppose it is the right thing to do."

"Of course it is." He rewarded her with the warm smile that she knew would continue to have the power to thrill her long after this mock marriage had ended. "You've got to learn to trust your husband, Sasha."

"I do." Even though she knew he was joking, the idea was a pleasant one. It continued to comfort her during their time in the police station. And while they deposited the gambling check in her meager savings account.

"I'm so sorry about your suit," she murmured as they drove back to the apartment.

Mitch shrugged off her concern. "I don't have that many occasions to wear one, anyway."

"But you looked so handsome in it. I suppose the cleaner could dry it, but I'm afraid your trousers are ruined."

He glanced down at the long tear over his knee. "Next time, I'll have to remember to just run the perp down with my Batmobile."

Sasha smiled at the image. "You are talking about Batman, right? The American movie superhero."

He smiled back. "Got it on the first try."

Not wanting to embarrass him, Sasha refrained from adding that she considered Mitch her very personal superhero.

A comfortable silence settled over them. Mitch was the first to break it. "I think we did okay with Potter. Though I sure wasn't expecting a pop quiz."

"Neither was I." Sasha's tone turned gloomy at the memory.

"I felt like a contestant on 'The Newlywed Game.' With a lot more at stake than a side-by-side refrigerator. At least I could answer what side of the bed each of us sleeps on."

"I sleep on the right side," she said promptly. "You sleep on the left."

"That's what I said," he agreed.

She exhaled a sigh of relief. "So, we got one right."

"How about favorite movie?" Mitch asked.

"That's easy." Despite the seriousness of their situation, Sasha grinned.

"Honeymoon in Vegas," they both said together.

"Favorite song?" Mitch asked.

"'Blue Hawaii.'" It hadn't been. But after last night's dream...

"Three for three," Mitch said as he stopped for a red light. "We're on a roll." It was then he made the mistake of glancing over at her. Their eyes held, each remembering the sensual dream. And their slumberous response to it. "I guess we didn't do so badly, after all."

"I guess not." Her voice was soft and throaty and strummed innumerable emotional chords. "At least we managed to stall the final decision until Mr. Donald O. Potter's home visit."

"Won't that just be a barrel of laughs." Mitch would rather invite Ghengis Khan to the apartment than let Potter cross his threshold. He idly considered digging a moat and filling it with bureaucrat-eating alligators.

"I don't suppose we could bar the doors and windows and pour boiling oil down on him?" Sasha suggested.

Mitch laughed. Pleased they were thinking along the same lines, he reached out and ruffled her hair in a casual, friendly gesture. "Sweetheart, I do like your style."

The light turned green. But the mood had been lightened enough that Mitch regained his confidence about pulling off the marriage charade.

Working together, they could fool Potter. And any other obnoxious bureaucrats the government might send their way. But as he approached the apartment building and viewed the familiar car parked at the curb, he realized that he and Sasha were about to undergo a test far more rigid than anything the United States government could come up with.

"What's wrong?" she asked, hearing his muttered curse.

"Better brace yourself, Sasha, darlin'," Mitch said with a long sigh as he pulled into his parking space, "because you're about to meet your new mother-in-law."

The moment she saw Margaret Cudahy, Sasha knew where Mitch had gotten his good looks.

Vivid blue eyes that were twins of her son's swept over him, from the top of his wet head down to his soaked shoes. "Mitchel Cudahy, what on earth have you gotten into now?"

"It's a long story. And not very interesting."

"That's what you said while the ER nurse was pulling cactus needles out of your rear end last week," she retorted. "Lord, if it weren't for Lady Clairol, my hair would be as white as snow. However, you may be right. I'm probably better off not knowing."

She shook her head with maternal chagrin, then changed the subject. "I was about to scold you for eloping without telling your mother. However—" she gave Sasha a genuine warm smile and a quick hug "—I'm so happy to have a new daughter that I can't work up all that much irritation."

"Mom, this is Sasha." To Sasha's surprise, her all-American hero began shuffling his foot in the pile of the carpet. "Sasha, this is my mother."

"Hello, Mrs. Cudahy," Sasha said. She began to extend her hand, but decided the gesture was too formal after that hug. "It is nice to meet you."

"It's a delight to meet you, Sasha." Her warm smile seconded her words. "And please, you must call me Margaret. Or, perhaps when we become closer, you might want to call me Mom."

It was, Sasha thought, a wonderfully American word. "I think I would like that."

Her mother's death had left a terrible void in her life. And although she knew that getting emotionally close to this open-hearted woman would be a huge mistake, Sasha found the idea of friendship with Mitch's mother undeniably appealing.

"So would I." The smile flashed again, warmer and wider, revealing a dimple high on Margaret's tanned cheek. "Jake has told me so many wonderful things about you, dear."

"Jake is a very nice man."

"He is, isn't he?" Margaret nodded. "He's been a wonderful husband to Katie." She smiled at Mitch. "It seems both my children have married well."

Mitch felt as if he'd just stepped into quicksand and was in danger of getting sucked in up to his neck. "That's probably because you and Pop set such a good example," he said, cringing inwardly as he wondered what his mother would say when she discovered the details of his marriage to Sasha.

"Your father was a wonderful husband," Margaret said. Her blue eyes became reminiscent. "It's too bad you didn't have a chance to meet him, Sasha. He would have been so happy to see his son happily married."

"He was a fireman, yes?" Sasha remembered Jake having mentioned that.

"That's right. We met after he was brought into the hospital for smoke inhalation." She sighed. "Although I could barely see his face through all the soot, it was love at first sight."

"I didn't know you were a nurse," Sasha said.

"I've worked the past thirty-three years in the emergency room at St. Joseph's," Margaret revealed proudly. "These days, of course, it's been upgraded to a trauma center."

Sasha liked knowing that she and Margaret had something in common besides Mitch. "I was a surgical nurse. In Russia," she revealed.

"I didn't know that." Mitch looked at Sasha with surprise. He'd assumed she'd waited tables in her native country.

Margaret's intelligent eyes narrowed at her son's unexpected comment. Sasha and Mitch both breathed a sigh of relief when she did not comment. "How are your licensing efforts coming along?" she asked Sasha.

"It's been difficult, because I've been moving around so much."

"Yes." Margaret nodded. "Jake also told me about your father. I'm sorry you're having such a troublesome time."

"I won a great deal of money while we were in Laughlin. Enough to hire a new detective."

"Well, isn't that lucky? And what a good omen for your marriage." She smiled at Mitch, who felt the guilty color rising from his collar.

"Meanwhile, why don't I see what I can do about getting you enrolled in a licensing school? I belong to several professional groups. I'm sure we can facilitate getting your papers processed. In fact, classes are beginning next week, I believe."

Mitch's mother's words made Sasha's heart soar. To be doing what she loved again, to be caring for people and helping them get well, was a glorious prospect!

"That would be very nice of you. But I wouldn't want to take advantage—"

"Nonsense, dear," Margaret said with that same brisk, cheerful attitude that made her such an excellent charge nurse, "that's what family's for."

Feeling horribly guilty about the charade they were perpetuating on this warmhearted woman, Sasha looked away. When her gaze met Mitch's, she could tell she was not the only one experiencing more than a twinge of conscience.

"Did you stop by for a reason, Mom?" Mitch asked as silence settled over the trio.

"Well, of course I wanted to meet your bride. And to invite you both to dinner Friday night. I'd dearly love to have you sooner, but there's been an outbreak of flu among the staff, so I'm working double shifts the next couple of days."

If there was one thing Mitch didn't want to do it was spend an entire evening being cross-examined by his mother. As much as he dearly loved her, Margaret Katherine Cudahy could be like a pit bull terrier with a bone. She'd want to know everything about Sasha and his courtship. And since he wasn't prepared to tell her the unvarnished truth, Mitch decided avoiding the issue was the prudent thing to do.

"Sorry, but I'm due back at work tomorrow. Which means I'll be on duty until midnight Friday night."

"You're returning to work so soon?" Margaret arched a chestnut brow. "I suppose I can understand your elopement," she said in a tone that suggested just the opposite, "but surely you're planning to take some sort of honeymoon? Something longer than a single night in Laughlin."

"Of course," Mitch said quickly.

Too quickly, he realized an instant later as his mother gave him one of those pointed looks he remembered too well from childhood: an omniscient mother stare that made a guy realize he'd never get away with a thing—no matter how old he might be.

"But everything was so unexpected, there wasn't time to rearrange the schedule."

"I suppose that makes sense."

"It's true," Mitch and Sasha said at the same time. They exchanged faint, conspiratory smiles, acknowledging that once again they were on the same wavelength. A smile that did not go unnoticed by the third member of the family.

"Well, all the more reason for Sasha to come to dinner," Margaret decided briskly. "You can't leave your bride all alone so soon after the wedding, Mitchel. In fact, a wonderful idea just occurred to me."

Mitch realized that he was not the only liar in the Cudahy family. His mother was one of those people who never began a day without a detailed list. Although she could shift gears with the best of them in her beloved ER, it was not like her to make a suggestion off the top of her head.

"What idea is that, Mom?"

"Katie and I can throw Sasha a bridal shower Friday night."

"A shower?" Mitch and Sasha asked at the same time. Her expression displayed a lack of understanding; his revealed something close to horror.

"It's a party most girls get before their wedding," Margaret explained to Sasha. "But by rushing you off to Laughlin, Mitch cheated you out of a traditional American experience. So, what time do you get off work?"

Sasha ignored the vibrations radiating from Mitch, who she realized wanted her to reject the idea. But his mother was so nice, and it had been so long since she'd been to any kind of party, she said, "I always work until closing on Friday. Which is usually a little after ten o'clock."

"Fine. Fortunately, Katie's baby is still at the age she's able to sleep anytime, anywhere." She walked toward the door, then turned and looked thoughtfully at Sasha. "It will be late in the evening when you finish work and I live quite a distance from the diner. Perhaps it would be more convenient for you if we have the shower here?" She looked questioningly at Mitch and Sasha, but did not wait for an answer.

"It's settled, then." She rubbed her hands with satisfaction. "We'll take care of all the preparations, dear, so all you have to do is show up. And have a good time."

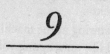

9

THE PHONE RANG just as his mother left the apartment. It seemed one of the crew had called in sick, Mitch told Sasha. He was needed as a replacement.

Although she smiled and pretended to understand, she could not miss his relief at having an excuse to escape. A little afraid that he'd lied to spare her feelings, that he was really intending to visit his lover, Sasha sighed and reminded herself that she'd gone into this relationship with her eyes wide open.

Trying to make herself useful, she decided to do the wash. Mitch had told her that he sent his laundry out, something she considered a terrible waste. "Besides," she told herself as she gathered up the soiled clothes from the bathroom hamper and put them in the laundry bag, "if I save him money and show him how useful I can be, perhaps he will not regret his decision so much."

Sasha found the apartment complex laundry room without any trouble. She poured in the detergent and, following instructions, started the washing machine.

Afraid to leave the clothes unguarded, she sat in the uncomfortable plastic chair, pleased to discover someone had left behind a glossy woman's magazine. She picked it up and immediately became immersed in the joys of cooking for the man you love.

It wasn't until she realized that her feet were wet that Sasha looked up from the pages of the magazine.

"Oh, no!"

She jumped up, staring at the machine that was belching soapsuds. It looked like an erupting volcano spewing foamy white lava. When she opened the lid to peer inside, more suds drooled thickly over the porcelain rim, down the sides and over the floor. Slamming it shut, Sasha felt a surge of panic.

She yanked the plug, stopping the machine in mid cycle. Then, slowly, tentatively, peeked beneath the lid again.

"Hello?" a woman's voice called from the door of the laundry room. "Is anyone in there?" Sasha heard the sound of high heels tapping on the vinyl floor, then a surprised gasp.

"Good heavens," Meredith Roberts exclaimed. "What on earth happened?"

"I was doing a wash," Sasha inwardly groaned at the idea of Mitch's lover—former lover, she hoped—catching her in such an undignified situation. "I don't understand what went wrong..."

"Well, here's your problem." Meredith picked up the box of detergent. "It's super-concentrated. You used too much."

"Oh." Sasha's spirits sagged. "I didn't know."

Meredith shrugged shoulders clad in an expensive and very stylish fuchsia and turquoise silk jacket. "I imagine things are a bit different in Russia."

"How do you know I'm Russian?"

"Well, even if Mitch hadn't told me all about you, your accent is a sure giveaway. You sound just like Natasha."

It was the same thing Ben Houston had told her. "That's a cartoon, right?"

"A very good one," Meredith agreed. "Although I'm not certain you'd find it all that flattering. I'm Meredith Roberts, by the way."

"I know. I've seen you on television. And in the diner."

"After the fire," Meredith agreed. "I remember wanting to interview you, but the owner didn't want the negative publicity."

"She was trying to protect me. Since I'm the one who started the fire."

"I got the impression that's what she was doing." Meredith surprised Sasha by taking off her pumps and stockings and wading barefoot through the suds. "Let's get your wash into another machine to finish it," she suggested. "Then I'd like to talk with you for a while."

Worried that Meredith was going to demand her right to Mitch's attention, Sasha didn't answer, but watched unhappily as the chic woman opened the washer.

"Uh-oh."

"What now?"

"I don't recall Mitch owning pink underwear."

Sasha viewed the bright pink cotton briefs Meredith was holding up—briefs that had been white when she'd put them into the washer—then groaned as she sank down onto the chair again.

"I must have accidently mixed my red blouse in with the whites. Mitch will be furious."

"It's no big deal." Meredith sat down beside her. "Just buy him some more. He'll never know."

"I do not want to lie to my husband. A marriage should be based on honesty."

Meredith gave her a puzzled look. "Mitch told me this marriage was a green card scam."

"Mitch has talked with you? About our marriage?"

"Of course. He came by my place to explain the situation the day you two got back from your little trip to Laughlin." When she realized that her words seemed to cause Sasha even more misery, she sighed. "Oh, hell." She gave Sasha a long look. "You're in love with him, aren't you?"

Sasha opened her mouth to lie, but she couldn't. Not about this. "Yes," she admitted.

"Well." Meredith reached into her purse, pulled out a pack of cigarettes and, ignoring the No Smoking sign on the wall, lit up. "Imagine that."

Since she had no answer to that enigmatic statement, Sasha said nothing.

"You know, that explains a lot," Meredith said finally.

"What do you mean?"

"He seemed edgy after your elopement."

"I imagine it was difficult for him. Explaining why he hadn't told you his plans ahead of time."

"Mitch and I never had any claims on one another," Meredith assured her. "I was surprised, but not particularly upset. Although he seemed to be."

Sasha had to ask. "Perhaps he loves you?"

Meredith laughed at that. "Honey, what Mitch and I shared had absolutely nothing to do with love." Realizing what she'd said, and to whom, her grin was replaced by a frown. "I'm sorry. I was out of line."

"No." It was Sasha's turn to smile. "To be truthful, I'm relieved to hear that the relationship between you and Mitch wasn't serious." She sighed. "Unfortunately, that doesn't mean his relationship with me is."

Meredith exhaled a long stream of blue smoke. "I wouldn't bet on that."

"I am not the kind of wife a man like Mitch needs."

The newswoman lifted a brow. "And what kind is that?"

"A woman who knows how to cook his meals. A woman who would not turn his underwear pink."

This time Meredith's laugh was loud and long. "Sweetheart," she said, tossing the word off with the same casualness Mitch was accustomed to using, "the domestic goddess route of catching a husband went out of style the day men discovered sex."

She stubbed out the cigarette in a foam cup left behind by an earlier visitor to the laundry room, crossed her legs, and said, "Let's talk about your search for your father. There's no telling how much help some free publicity might be. Then we can discuss ways to save your marriage."

If anyone had told her she'd been seeking romance advice from her husband's lover, Sasha would have said they were crazy. Yet somehow it seemed strangely right.

Reminding herself that her marriage had been unconventional from the start, she sat back in the chair, ignored the melting soapsuds and began to talk.

"YOU KNOW, HONEY, you didn't have to come into work today," Glory said when Sasha arrived at the diner that afternoon.

"I'm grateful to have something to occupy my mind."

"Having second thoughts, are you?"

Sasha thought about her father; about how far she'd already come; about how she refused to return to Russia without at least having met this man who'd contributed half of everything she was. And so much of what her children someday would be.

"Mitch was right. Marriage was the only practical solution to my problem."

"It's not going to be easy," the older woman warned.

"Convincing Mr. Donald O. Potter that our marriage is real?"

"No." Glory's eyes warmed with sympathy. "Convincing yourself that it isn't."

As usual, Glory was right.

Trusting her friend's judgment, Sasha showed the cook a recipe from the laundry room magazine and explained her plan to win him over with gourmet fare.

"I don't know," Glory muttered as she studied the instructions for flambéing chicken breasts with warmed apricot brandy. "Mitch has always been pretty much a steak-and-potatoes man from what I can tell."

"But this dinner looked very good in the pictures."

"I'm sure it did. But in case you've forgotten, honey, you weren't exactly born with a white thumb. Last time you tried frying a few pieces of bacon, you managed to set my kitchen on fire."

"There isn't any bacon in this recipe."

"Well, that may be, but believe me, Sasha, a woman with all you've got going for you doesn't have to worry about slaving away in the kitchen. Not when your husband would rather have you in the bedroom."

Sasha blushed as her friend and employer unknowingly echoed Meredith Roberts's words. "That is too easy, for Mitch. He doesn't have any trouble getting women into his bed. I want to show him I have more to offer."

"I'm still not sure it's a good plan," Glory said worriedly. "How about I help out and cook it for you?"

"That would be cheating. I want to do it myself."

Glory shook her head. "Since it doesn't look as if I can change your mind, why don't you go on home right now? Then you can surprise Mitch with your fancy dinner at the station."

"But you need me for the dinner shift."

"No problem. You know my niece Amber?"

"The one who was in here last week to talk with you? The pretty one who just graduated from high school?"

"That's her. She's putting herself through college and can always use a few extra bucks. I'll call and have her come down to fill in for you." The older woman gave Sasha a hug. "Now, scoot."

Sasha returned to the apartment loaded down with plastic grocery bags. Although her shallots and mushrooms did not end up possessing the same geometric perfection as the magazine photographs, Sasha was relieved when she managed to get them cut into pieces without slicing off a finger.

She browned them in the extra-virgin olive oil, as instructed, keeping the heat turned low.

So far, so good.

She was transferring the mushrooms and shallots from the frying pan to a plate for safekeeping, when the mixture, helped along by its oil coating, slid off the plate onto the floor.

"Damn." Sasha cursed first in Russian, then English.

Glancing around, as if looking for spies, she picked up the spilled pieces and put them back on the plate. After all, the floor was clean. And she didn't want to return to the store where she would be faced with another dizzying array of American consumer goods.

Although her boned chicken breasts did not look anything like the perfect, almost heart-shaped ones depicted in the magazine, she managed to cook them to a lovely golden brown shade without any further problems. Meanwhile, she had the brandy warming in a saucepan on a nearby burner, just as instructed.

After returning the mushrooms and shallots to the copper-bottomed frying pan, she poured the heated apricot brandy over the mixture, struck a match and lit it.

There was a roar, sounding like a rushing wind, and an explosion. Sasha cried out as blue flames shot up to the ceiling, engulfing the frying pan and its carefully prepared contents.

MITCH WAS IN the station exercise room, punching the lights out of the canvas weight bag he imagined as Donald O. Potter's face when the shrill sound of the alarm shattered the lazy afternoon silence.

As the familiar adrenaline shot through him, he yanked off the padded leather gloves and raced toward the truck, pulling on his protective gear as he ran.

Emergency lights flashing, the truck tore through the streets, dodging traffic, slowing at intersections, picking up speed to career around corners. Despite the seriousness of his work, riding on the back of the truck, leaning into the curves, the siren blaring in his ears, was a high that always left Mitch grinning.

By the time the red truck pulled up in front of his apartment building, Mitch was no longer smiling. When he realized that the smoke was pouring out the window of his apartment, his blood chilled.

"Dammit!" he shouted to Jake as he jumped down from the truck. "Sasha could be in there!"

Before anyone could remind him that he was going against procedure, he ran up the outside stairs, his heart pounding in his throat, terrified at what horror might await him.

Whatever he'd been expecting, it was definitely not what he found.

Sasha was standing in the middle of the small kitchen. Everything around her—the cupboards, the countertops, the floor, as well as herself—was covered with foam. The ceiling was charred, though most of the smoke had dissipated. She was frozen, like a marble statue, the large red fire extinguisher still held out in front of her like a shield.

"Sasha?" Lingering fear made his voice little more than a croak. "What the hell happened here?"

"Mitch?" She turned toward him, her face as white as the foam, her wide brown eyes dominating her pale face. "Oh, Mitch!"

Relieved to see him, looking wonderfully like that glorious hero she'd first fallen in love with, Sasha dropped the extinguisher and hurled herself into his arms.

"I was s-so frightened! It happened so fast. One minute everything was fine, then the next minute, wh-whoosh! And then the room filled up with smoke and the smoke d-detector started blaring and I didn't know what to do, so I called 911, because I was afraid I was going to b-burn down the building.

"But then I remembered the fire extinguisher beneath the sink and I tried to spray it on the pan, but it was very hard to hold steady with all that foam spraying out of it, and now I've made the most horrible mess of your lovely clean kitchen!" She finished on a wail.

If she hadn't been so damn upset, Mitch would have laughed. He rubbed away some dissolving foam so he could press his lips against her temple. "You know, sweetheart, we really have to stop meeting like this."

In answer, she wrapped her arms around him tighter and buried her face in his heavy coat. From the way her shoulders were shaking, and the strangled sounds she was making, Mitch realized that his words, which had been meant as a joke, had instead made her cry.

"Honey, I'm sorry. I didn't mean to hurt your feelings." He ran his hand, which suddenly felt too large and clumsy, down her foam-slick hair in an ineffectual attempt to soothe.

"Please don't cry," he begged as he felt her hitch in another of those deep, shuddering breaths. "It's going to be all right. I promise."

"Oh, Mitch." She lifted her face, which was streaked with soot and tears. "I truly am sorry." Her words dissolved on a breathless little giggle that amazed him. "I was trying to cook a dinner to bring to you. But instead my dinner brought you to me!"

She wiped at the moisture streaming down her blackened cheeks with the backs of her hands. "Do you have any idea how funny you looked, charging in to rescue me?"

It was a direct hit to his ego. Mitch was not accustomed to women laughing at him. But as he thought back on how he had played hotshot, leaving the rest of the crew and kicking in his own door, he could see the humor in their situation.

"Funny? I looked funny?" His smile took the objection from his words.

"Funny," she agreed. "But also very dashing."

"That's better." He put a palm against her cheek. "You are," he said with a deep, low chuckle, "the only woman I have ever known who uses a smoke alarm as a cooking timer."

Her laughter reminded him of sunshine. Champagne. Music. "I wanted to surprise you."

His chuckle deepened as he dove his hands into her hair and tilted her grinning smoke-stained face up to his. "Well, darlin', if that was your goal, you sure as hell succeeded."

They were both laughing as their lips met and clung.

"Sorry," Jake drawled as he entered the kitchen, "looks as if you two newlyweds don't need any help here."

Immersed in their blissful, smoky kiss, neither Mitch nor Sasha answered.

Neither did they notice the man who'd entered the kitchen behind Jake.

"What the hell is going on here?" the all-too-familiar voice demanded.

Sasha and Mitch turned, observed a rigidly angry Donald O. Potter standing amid the foam covering the floor, and burst out laughing.

10

AFTER MITCH HAD LEFT with the firemen, and Potter had returned to whatever rock he spent his time away from the office lurking beneath, Sasha got busy with buckets and mops and sponges and cleaned up the mess she'd made.

Although the task was not the least bit pleasant, she couldn't stop smiling. The sweet kiss she and Mitch had shared lingered in her mind and on her lips. Even Mr. Donald O. Potter's unexpected arrival could not dampen the happiness that lighthearted moment had instilled.

After muttering something about the government not having a policy about inviting firebugs into the country, Potter had stomped off in a snit. At the time, Mitch claimed he was undoubtedly angry about having stumbled into their lives at a particularly romantic moment. Now he'd have difficulty reporting back to his superiors that their marriage was a scam.

Which, of course, it was. But the more Sasha thought about it, the more she knew that they belonged together. She could make Mitch happy.

"So long as I do not burn down his house first," she amended as she stood beneath the streaming shower, washing the foam and soot down the drain.

By the time she finally crawled into bed, she was exhausted. Hugging Mitch's pillow, which carried his scent, she drifted off into a deep sleep resplendent with romantic dreams of her dashing husband.

ALTHOUGH SASHA'S BRIDAL shower might be after the fact, and the only guests were Mitch's mother and sister and Glory, who closed the diner early for the festivities—she'd never had a more wonderful time.

The conversation flowed easily and unsurprisingly centered mostly around men. As the night grew later and the champagne continued to flow, the stories grew more intimate and the jokes more bawdy, making Sasha feel as if she must be the only twenty-four-year-old virgin left in the world.

"Are you sure it was the right thing to do?" she asked Margaret for the umpteenth time that evening. "Agreeing to tell my story on television?"

"It couldn't hurt," Margaret assured her. "And who knows, perhaps someone who sees the newscast will know your father."

Since her quest had been fruitless so far, Sasha wasn't holding out a lot of hope for this latest effort. "I should have asked Mitch." Ever since Meredith had left with her cameraman, Sasha's doubts had grown like billowing smoke from a forest fire.

"I don't know how marriages work in Russia," Katie said, "but here in America, women don't need to get permission from their husbands for every little thing they do."

Sasha had liked Mitch's sister on first sight. Part of that, she realized, was due to the woman's striking resemblance to her brother, but mostly she liked her because she was warm and outgoing. And seemed genuinely interested in Sasha's dilemma.

"Appearing on television is more than a little thing," Sasha argued. Especially since..." Her worried voice drifted off as she realized she'd been about to reveal the status of their marriage.

"Especially since your marriage to my son is supposed to be only one of convenience?" Margaret asked, slanting her a sideways glance as she cut the white-tiered wedding cake Sasha had been deprived of by eloping.

Sasha could feel the damning color flooding into her face. "You know about that?"

"It wasn't that difficult to figure out," Katie said. "My brother has specialized in hit-and-run relationships since he was fifteen. Then he suddenly runs off and gets married to a woman who just happens to be embroiled in immigration problems. And we're expected to buy that story?"

"That's the same thing Mr. Donald O. Potter said," Sasha admitted. "You must think I'm a terrible person to be part of such a deceitful scheme."

"Of course we don't think you're a terrible person," Margaret said.

"But that may be because we also know something that hateful Mr. Potter doesn't," Katie added.

"What is that?"

"That Mitch is in love with you, of course," Margaret answered mildly.

If only that were true! Sasha sighed and decided she must be totally honest with this kindhearted woman. "I am afraid you're mistaken."

"Not according to Jake," Katie said, rising from the couch when the baby, Megan, started whimpering in the bedroom. "He says he's never seen Mitch so distracted as he's been since you two got back from Laughlin."

Sasha was surprised. And pleased. "I distract Mitch?" she asked when Katie returned with Mitch's two-month-old niece.

"I think his exact words were 'bothered and bewildered.'" Katie grinned as she unbuttoned her blouse and put her daughter to her breast.

As she watched the infant's rosebud mouth begin to suckle, Sasha felt an unexpected maternal tug deep inside her.

"That's the same way I feel about Mitch."

"There, you see?" Margaret began passing out the pieces of cake. "You're made for each other. Because believe me, Sasha, my son has never let any woman get under his skin. Or into his heart, until you."

Sasha thought about that a moment. "He says it is just physical attraction."

"That's what he'd like to believe," Katie said with an amused laugh that shook her chest and made the baby complain for a moment. "And although I love my brother to pieces, for a bright guy, when it comes to love and romance, he's as dense as every other male on the planet. So, it's going to be up to you to prove him wrong."

The idea was enormously appealing. "How do I do that?"

"Seduce him," the other three women in the room said at the same time. They laughed at Sasha's expression, which was equal parts shock, embarrassment and interest.

"Mitch's father was a confirmed bachelor," Margaret revealed. "But the moment I met him, I knew he was the man for me. Poor Garrett didn't know what hit him." Mitch's mother's smile was warmly reminiscent. "We were married two weeks after we met."

"I tried the same thing with Jake," Katie said. "Of course, either he was more resistant than Pops, or I was more impatient. Because after three months, when he still hadn't caved in, I proposed to him."

"You asked Jake to marry you?"

Katie shrugged off Sasha's incredulous response. "I loved him. He loved me. Marriage seemed the next logical step."

"My son may have gotten the order a bit reversed, Sasha," Margaret allowed, "by getting married, then falling in love. But that doesn't change the fact that Mitch is in love with you, dear. Anyone can tell by the way he looks at you and by the way his voice changes when he talks to you. Or about you."

"And the way he threatened to beat up Jake for suggesting that any other man might want you," Katie added.

"Mitch threatened to hit Jake? Because of me?"

"After he mentioned wanting to personally murder a bunch of Shriners."

The idea was incredible. And wonderful.

"There is one problem," Sasha said reluctantly.

"What's that?" Margaret asked.

"I don't have any idea how to seduce a man. Especially one as experienced as Mitch."

"Don't worry about that," Katie said. "You've put yourself in the hands of experts."

"And the first thing any woman needs going into battle," Glory said with a deep, knowing chuckle as she handed Sasha the box wrapped in white paper embossed with silver bows, "is the appropriate artillery."

It seemed that all the women had had the same idea. Every one of the gifts were frothy bits of satin and lace designed to appeal to a man's sexual fantasies.

"I don't think I have the nerve to wear this," Sasha murmured, taking a sheer black lace catsuit from a layer of tissue paper wrapping.

"Sure you do," Katie assured her. "Just make certain you have a lot of protection handy. It's because of an outfit just like that one that Jake and I have Megan."

Once again Sasha blushed as the others laughed. Despite the raised voices, after being burped, little Megan fell back to sleep, happily satiated.

A short time later, a few minutes after midnight, a knock came on the door. Sasha opened the door and was terrified to see a uniformed policeman standing there.

"Sorry, ma'am," he said, his stern expression reminding her of every policeman she'd ever feared back in Russia, "but we've received a complaint of noise coming from this apartment."

"I'm sorry," she managed to get out through lips that had gone as dry as dust. "We did not mean to be too loud. I promise we will be more quiet." Although the other day's encounter with the police had not been unpleasant she didn't think she would ever outgrow the instinctive fear such a uniform instilled.

"I'm afraid that's not good enough, ma'am," he said, stepping past her into the apartment. The others watched expectantly as he crossed the room to the stereo. Sasha was surprised when he turned the volume even louder.

She was flabbergasted when he suddenly ripped off his uniform, revealing an amazingly tanned and toned body clad only in a skimpy pair of underwear adorned with a gleaming badge in a most inappropriate place. As he began to gyrate his hips, the women—Margaret Cudahy included—roared at Sasha's shocked expression and began to clap in time to the driving beat of the music.

AT FIRST, a night on the town after his shift ended had seemed like a good idea. After all, Mitch assured himself, since Sasha was having her own party, she wouldn't be expecting him home anytime soon. Besides, the idea of facing his mother, sister and Glory—who'd be watching him like a wiggling bug stuck to a corkboard with a pin, to ensure he was treating his new bride properly—was enough to make him want to run off and join the French foreign legion the way Gary Cooper had in *Beau Geste,* which still showed up on late night cable every once in a while.

Even if his and Sasha's marriage wasn't real, a bachelor party was a time-honored American tradition. That being the case, who was he to deprive the guys at the firehouse of an opportunity to party?

The only problem, Mitch realized as he sat at a table at the French Cabaret—a Club for Gentlemen—nursing his first beer of the night was that he wasn't having a good time. The platinum-blond stripper lying on her back on the stage peeling black mesh stockings down her long, long legs was undeniably gorgeous. And her remarkable breast enhancement alone must have paid for some local plastic surgeon's new boat.

Although she was doing her best to entertain, with sultry looks, bold smiles and saucy tosses of her long spiral curls, he couldn't help thinking about how sexy Sasha had looked, sitting at the roulette table in that ridiculously short denim skirt. And how her breasts, beneath the virginal white cotton nightgown had felt so soft, so inviting.

The stripper's seductive smile didn't fade in the slightest when a drunk down at the end of the bar began shouting raucous suggestions as she dispensed with the second stocking. But when she stood up again, she moved a little bit closer to the table occupied by Mitch, Jake, and three other firemen from Ladder Company No. 13.

Unfortunately, when she leaned forward, meeting Mitch's eyes, and licked her glossy crimson lips with her tongue, it was Sasha's mouth Mitch immediately imagined tasting. It was Sasha's kiss he found himself fantasizing about yet again.

"Damn."

Jake shot him a look. "So, which is it? Are you regretting the fact that you shouldn't go home with the luscious Miss April Luv? Or are you were wishing you were home with your bride?"

"She's not my bride," Mitch muttered as one of the fire fighters, rising to the sensual invitation in those heavily lashed, kohl-lined eyes, slipped a five dollar bill in the woman's sequined G-string. Mitch took a long pull on the brown beer bottle. "Not really."

Before Jake could argue, the stripper leaned down toward him. "How about you, bachelor boy?" she cooed, revealing that she'd overheard the earlier table conversation about the impromptu party. Although he'd like to think she found him irresistible, Mitch figured April Luv's real interest was that such occasions were undoubtedly good for a big tip.

She gave her silicone marvels an enthusiastic shimmy that sent her tassels swirling. "How about your own private table dance?" She was so close he could detect the faint odor of perspiration underlying the cloyingly sweet perfume. Her breasts were waving in his face like Old Glory on the Fourth of July. "So you'll have something to remember when you've settled into safe, boring domesticity."

As unpalatable as he found the idea of settling down, Mitch still found himself unmoved by Miss April's charms. He was just about to hand over the dough and forego the private attention, when the obnoxious drunk suddenly pushed his way between Mitch and the stripper to grab fistfuls of those voluptuous, offered breasts.

April Luv let loose with a stream of swear words that could have made a longshoreman blush. The drunk, angered by the invective tried to climb onto the stage while the stripper attempted to discourage him by stomping on his hairy-backed hands with her high heels.

Mitch quickly glanced around looking for the bouncer who'd been standing guard at the door when they'd arrived. Unfortunately the muscle-bound giant was nowhere to be seen.

Which left Mitch no other choice. Acting on instinct, cursing ripely, he leapt up, tipping over his wooden chair, and threw himself onto the drunken assailant's back.

The cretin's buddies staggered to their feet, fists flailing, and naturally, the other members of Ladder Company No. 13 rose to the challenge.

It took less than thirty seconds for the attraction between the drunk, the stripper and Mitch to turn into a full-fledged brawl. By the time Mitch heard the familiar sound of sirens, four chairs had been broken, six noses bloodied and the drunk who had started all the fun lay on the floor below the stage, the victim of a well-placed punch, a shimmering tassel clutched in one fist.

11

MITCH ARRIVED HOME with a rapidly swelling eye, in a rotten mood from having had to talk his way out of being arrested. He was not at all pleased to discover Sasha handcuffed to a buffed-up guy with a tanning salon bronzed body who was the male equivalent of Miss April Luv.

Fortunately, his mother efficiently herded everyone from the apartment, leaving Mitch and Sasha alone.

"Well," Mitch said finally, "I guess your party, at least, was a success."

"I had a very good time." Her worried gaze swept over his face, lingering on the horrid discoloration circling his right eye. "It seems you did not."

"No." That, he decided, had to be the understatement of the year. "I didn't."

"Did you get hurt fighting a fire?"

"No." His answer was brusque, discouraging further discussion.

Sasha waited for Mitch to elaborate. When he didn't, she glanced down at his hands and said, "We must tend to your wounds."

Amazingly, the discomfort of facing his mother, sister and wife with the evidence of the brawl on his face and hands had made Mitch forget all about his scraped knuckles. "It's no big deal."

"Mitch." Her tone was soft, but surprisingly firm. "I am a nurse. I'm also your wife. It is my duty to take care of your injuries."

The issue settled as far as she was concerned, Sasha headed toward the bathroom where she'd seen a bottle of hydrogen peroxide in the medicine chest.

Mitch shrugged, then followed her. He leaned against the doorjamb and watched as she lined up the bottle, some soap and a stack of gauze squares with an intensity that suggested she was preparing to perform open heart surgery right on that faux marble countertop.

"I've never heard you talk like that."

"Like what?"

"I don't know." He hesitated. "Kind of bossy, I guess."

"I'm sorry if you don't like it, but—"

"Actually, I think I do."

"Really?"

"Yeah." The more he thought about it, the more he found this new aspect of Sasha's personality interesting. "I guess I've been thinking of you as poor, beleaguered little Sasha for so long, I never considered the fact that you might have had a different sort of life in Russia."

The portrait he painted was far from flattering. And regrettably true. Sasha decided that it was time she stopped behaving like a victim. She'd graduated at the head of her class and had been a highly respected surgical nurse. She'd overcome miles of red tape to come to this country. As nice as it was to have Mitch coming to her rescue every time she turned around, it was time for her to begin fighting her own battles.

"Different," she agreed mildly, "but not necessarily better. Although I do miss nursing. Which is why I'll be very grateful to your mother for anything she can do to facilitate my licensing." She gestured toward the closed commode. "Sit down and I'll take care of your cuts."

"Yes, ma'am." With a ghost of a smile playing at the corners of his lips, Mitch did as instructed.

Briskly and efficiently she washed the scraped skin with soap, trying to ignore the scents of cigarette smoke, beer and perfume that clung to his hair and clothing.

"It's not what you think," he said, noticing the faint wrinkling of her nose.

"I wasn't thinking anything."

"Sure you were. You think I've been brawling in some bar."

"Were you?" Drunken behavior was nothing new to Sasha. Since many men in Russia suffered from alcoholism, she'd witnessed the dangers of such overindulgence when they showed up injured at the hospital.

"Not exactly."

"I see," she said mildly as she rinsed his right hand beneath the faucet.

Surprised she wasn't going to push him for an explanation, Mitch felt the need to explain anyway. "Some of the guys wanted to take me out for a bachelor party. Kind of a male version of your bridal shower."

"How nice for you." She rinsed the left hand.

"Well, it should have been. But there was this drunk and he was bothering Miss April Luv, and—"

"You rushed in to rescue her." Sasha reminded herself that it was only Mitch's nature. It didn't mean that he had any romantic feelings for the woman with the sensual name.

Besides, she wasn't all that innocent herself, she admitted, thinking about how attractive she'd found the sexy pretend policeman. Even if he didn't stir her blood the way Mitch could with a single glance, or a warm smile.

"Someone had to do it," Mitch said grumpily. "Unfortunately, the bouncer was outside having a heart-to-heart conversation with a couple of bikers."

She had no idea what a bouncer was, did not know why he would feel the need to leave his post to talk with bicycle riders, but she did understand exactly how Mitch had received his injuries.

"She was fortunate you were there."

"The lucky thing was that one of the responding cops was Jake's cousin," he muttered, "or I'd be spending the night in jail."

"Don't be silly. They do not put heroes in jail."

He frowned as he remembered the stripper's enthusiastic kisses and her breathy declarations that he'd always be her knight in shining armor. "Believe me, Sasha, there's nothing the least bit heroic about bar fights."

"I believe Miss April Luv would see things differently." Sasha swabbed on the hydrogen peroxide with the sterile gauze.

"Does that hurt?" she asked when Mitch flinched.

"Not at all," he lied.

Knowing he was not telling the truth, she lifted his hand and blew softly on the stinging wounds.

Her breath was as soft as thistledown, as warm as summer sunshine. And it stirred emotions that Mitch knew were better left alone. But he'd never been one to stick to the safe or prudent path in life.

"I lied," he admitted.

"I know. But that's all right, Mitch." She blew on the other hand. "Many men have difficulty admitting to pain."

"I'm not talking about that. Well, maybe I did fudge the truth a little about how my hands felt, but I was referring to what I said earlier. About only seeing you as beleaguered and all that."

"Oh. You don't see me this way?"

"Actually, I do. I mean, I guess I did. But there was more I didn't say."

"Oh." She looked down at him. She saw the heat in his eyes, and with a shocked intake of breath tried to release his hand, but he stopped her by deftly lacing their fingers together.

"Don't you want to know what else I was thinking?" He lifted their joined hands to his lips and pressed a kiss against the inside of her wrist, causing her pulse to leap.

"Mitch . . ." Sasha was suddenly honestly afraid. Afraid of him. Afraid of herself. And terrified of having her heart broken.

Reminding herself of her new resolution to take charge of her life, she tried to tug her hand free. "I don't think this is a very good idea."

"What's wrong, Sasha?" His eyes were on hers as his wicked lips forged a fiery trail of sparks up her arm. "How can a husband telling his wife that he thinks she's about the sexiest, most desirable woman he's ever seen be a bad idea?"

Sexy? Desirable? Her heart soared at the long-awaited words.

"We're not really husband and wife."

"That's funny." When his tongue touched the crook of her elbow, desire pooled hotly between her legs. "I have a paper tucked away in my underwear drawer that says we are." He spread his legs and pulled her closer.

Heaven help her, she did not resist. Instead, Sasha found herself staring down at the buttons on his blood-stained shirt, struck with a sudden, almost overwhelming impulse to rip them all away.

"Our marriage is in name only," she protested. "That was what you proposed."

"True enough." Her skin was as soft as silk. Mitch wanted to touch her all over. Taste her all over. "But there's really nothing to prevent us from changing the terms of the deal, is there?"

Never had Sasha been so tempted. Never had she wanted a man so badly. And never had she loved anyone so deeply. Which was why, she warned herself, she must tread very carefully where Mitch Cudahy was concerned.

"There is one reason."

Her voice was so soft Mitch could barely hear her. "What's that, sweetheart?" he murmured, pulling her closer still so he could nuzzle his head against her abdomen.

It was that throwaway word that he tossed so casually to every woman he met that assured Sasha she was right to be cautious.

"You do not know me." It was the hardest decision she'd ever made. Sasha could only pray it was the right one. "And I do not know you."

"Hell, sweetheart," he argued, unwittingly driving another nail into the ragged wound he was making in her heart, "we know more about each other than a lot of people who tumble into bed together."

Unfortunately, Sasha realized that he was speaking from experience. "I realize many of the women you know take lovemaking lightly. But I am not most women, Mitch."

That firmness was back. In her voice and, as he looked up at her, in her steady brown gaze. Mitch sighed and reminded himself that bedding Sasha probably would have been a mistake, anyway. Every instinct he possessed told him this situation could get emotionally sticky.

"You're right." He released her, but the warmth of his touch, his gaze, continued to linger in her breast. "I'm sorry. I had no right to try to take advantage of you that way. No right to try to talk you into doing something you don't want to do."

Sasha experienced a moment of panic. This was not what she wanted! She'd only intended to stall long enough for them to get to know one another better. To give Mitch time to fall in love with her. So that when they ultimately did make love, he'd understand that they belonged together.

The one thing she didn't want to do was to encourage him to give up on her entirely!

She took a deep breath and, having no experience in how to maneuver in such tight emotional quarters, decided to follow her instincts and hope they'd lead her in the right direction.

"But I do want to make love to you, Mitch." There, she'd said it. "But it's more complicated than that."

"I don't understand. We're legally married. The mutual attraction—the chemistry—has been obvious from the beginning, Sasha. I want you and you want me. What's so complicated about that?"

Because I love you. And you don't love me. "I told you," she said, "I do not take sex lightly."

He nodded his approval. "That's wise. Especially in this day and age."

"Yes." She twisted her fingers together and tried again. "It's just that all this has happened so fast, Mitch. You and I, and our marriage. And winning all that money, and then the meeting with that horrid Mr. Donald O. Potter, and the purse stealer, and your mother..."

"All right." His lips quirked with a small smile and humor brightened his eyes as he held up his wounded hand. "I get the point, sweetheart. I don't need a blow-by-blow replay."

"Fine." Reminding herself once again that she was not the pitiful little wretch he thought he'd married, she tilted her chin and forced her runaway pulse to something resembling normalcy.

"We'll take our time," Mitch agreed. "And get to know one another." Personally, he'd always felt like bed was a dandy place to get to know a woman. But never having had to push, let alone coax a female between his sheets, he had no intention of beginning with Sasha.

"Thank you," she said. "And while we're being honest, may I request a favor?"

"Sure."

This time she managed to ignore the warmth of his smile. "I would appreciate it if you would stop calling me sweetheart."

That finally said, she swept from the room with a regal air that reminded Mitch of royalty. For a moment he was irked at being dismissed so coolly, then he threw back his head and laughed.

"So, WHAT DID YOU expect?" Jake asked the next day. He was spotting for Mitch, who was working off his frustration by lifting weights in the workout room at the station. "That just because you married the girl, she'd show her undying gratitude by leaping naked into your bed?"

"I wasn't looking for gratitude." Mitch grunted as he hefted the bar over his head. "I was looking for sex."

"Makes sense to me. I told you most men would love a chance to roll around in the hay with our little Sasha Mikhailova."

"She's Sasha Cudahy. At least for the time being. And I told you I don't want to hear about most men!" Mitch dropped the bar back down with a curse.

"Whooee." Jake grinned and held his hands up in a gesture of defeat. "Sounds like you've got it bad."

"That's ridiculous. I'm just horny." Mitch pushed the bar up again, irritation providing an extra burst of power. "You would be, too, if you'd gone a week without getting laid."

"Yeah. Like that never happens to the rest of us," Jake said dryly. "Wait until you've got a wife in the eighth month of pregnancy, pal. Our water bill went through the roof from all the cold showers I was taking."

"Since I'm leaving the responsibility of providing Mom with grandkids to you and Katie, I have no intention of ever experiencing that aspect of marriage," Mitch insisted. "And if I'd wanted a life of celibacy I would have joined an order of trappist monks instead of the fire department."

Jake added more weight to both ends of the bar. "Katie was telling me something about some home visit by Glory's squinty-eyed weasel. So, when is it scheduled?"

"I don't know. Apparently they surprise you. Like fire drills." The first one, when Potter had discovered them kissing in the kitchen, had been a bonus. Mitch didn't expect subsequent visits to go as smoothly.

"Oh." Jake rubbed his chin. "So you and your bride have to continue to live as normal newlyweds as much as possible, just in case the immigration police stop by in the middle of the night?"

"That's pretty much it," Mitch muttered, shoving the heavier bar up with a force born of frustration.

"Tough break." Jake steadied the barbell as Mitch's inner turmoil set it shaking. "Well, at least once the visit is over with, and Sasha has her green card, you can get on with your separate lives."

"Yeah. And let me tell you, I can't wait."

Mitch sat up, wiped his hand against his sweat-stained shirt and wondered when he'd become such a damn liar.

GLORY WAS WAITING with a question when Sasha arrived the next day at work. "How come you didn't tell me about Mitch's mother's offer to get you enrolled in a licensing school?" she demanded with a frown.

Sasha hadn't known how to break the news that she'd be leaving to her friend. "I was going to tell you about that."

"That sounds like a terrific deal," Glory said after Sasha had explained. "And I know how much you've missed working in the operating room. So what's the problem?"

"For one thing, I don't want to leave you without a waitress. Not after you were so nice to hire me."

At that Glory broke out laughing. "Honey, I think it's time for me to come clean with you. The reason my sister's girl Amber stopped by last week was to ask for a job. I told you she's putting herself through Phoenix College."

Sasha nodded.

"The problem is, I had to turn her down because I knew how badly you needed work. But now that you're married and your mother-in-law is going to get you into school—"

"But what if Mitch doesn't want to stay married?" Sasha asked. "Even if I didn't want to keep working, which I do, once we get our annulment, it will be necessary to support myself."

"By then you'll have your nursing license," Glory observed. "But I'll bet you dollars to doughnuts that Mitch won't want that annulment."

Sasha hoped that would be true.

THE NEXT WEEK went by smoothly enough. Which Mitch decided was probably due to Sasha's being at school on the days he was home, and his being at the station for three of those days and nights.

The first morning they actually shared together was Friday, a week after Sasha's bridal shower and Mitch's stripper-club brawl.

They were just finishing breakfast when Margaret dropped by.

"Good morning, dears," she said, studiously ignoring the black eye that was still evident on Mitch's face. After declining Sasha's offer of coffee, she said, "I was planning my day off when I realized that Sasha probably doesn't have a proper dress for tomorrow night."

"Tomorrow night?" Sasha turned toward him. "Mitch?"

Hell. With all he'd had on his mind lately, he'd forgotten all about the upcoming governor's awards banquet.

"I don't know if I'm going to go to that dinner, Mom," he hedged.

"Well, of course you are." Margaret waved his words away. "The governor," she told Sasha with maternal pride, "is going to give Mitchel a medal. And name him Arizona hero of the year."

"Really?" Sasha's face was glowing with something that horrifyingly appeared to be wifely pride as she turned toward him. "This is true, Mitch?"

"It's no big thing," he mumbled as he began tearing apart a paper napkin.

"On the contrary," Margaret corrected, "it is a very big deal. Your father won the same award, Mitch. You owe it to his memory to show up. Besides," she said, her friendly gaze returning to Sasha, "you'll be sitting up on the dais with the governor. What better opportunity to show off your new bride?"

As he mumbled something that sounded like agreement, Mitch could feel the quicksand closing in over his head.

12

"I CAN'T AFFORD to do much shopping," Sasha said as she drove to the mall with Margaret and Katie. "I should save my money to use to find my father."

"Of course you should," Katie said. "But you're a married woman now."

"And I know my son would want to spend whatever is necessary for you to look your best Saturday night," Margaret added as extra inducement.

Remembering how Mitch had sighed as he had handed over his credit card in Laughlin, Sasha wasn't as certain that he would approve of this shopping trip.

Ten minutes later, she was standing in front of a three-way mirror, staring in stunned disbelief at her reflection.

"Didn't I tell you?" Katie, who'd found the glittery lame cocktail dress in the chichi boutique, crowed. "As seduction artillery goes, that dress is decidedly lethal."

"It is definitely short," Sasha murmured. She'd lived with her legs for twenty-four years without realizing how long they were! The knife-pleated, baby-doll style dress, held up with thin glittery straps, ended a great deal closer to her waist than her knees. "And bright."

"Red is perfect for a fireman's wife," Katie argued. "And the color is dynamite with your dark hair."

The contrast was appealing, Sasha admitted secretly. Still,

she didn't think she'd have the nerve to leave the house in such a skimpy, sexy dress.

She turned to Margaret, hoping the older woman would suggest something more prudent. "What do you think?"

Mitch's mother's judicial gaze swept over the brief cocktail dress. "I think my son's a goner." She held out a pair of dangling crystal earrings. "Try these. They'll be perfect."

Outvoted and more than a little overwhelmed, Sasha did not resist as the pair dragged her from store to store, seemingly determined to push the limit on Mitch's credit card.

By the end of the day, when she returned to the apartment laden down with packages, Sasha decided she knew exactly how Cinderella must have felt when her fairy godmother had shown up with that sparkling new ball gown and pumpkin coach.

The transformation the two women had wrought had been nothing short of miraculous. Anticipation bubbled like sparkling champagne in her veins as Sasha contemplated seducing her husband.

MITCH WAS LATE and not in the best of moods when he arrived home Saturday night from the station.

Although he'd left with time to spare to stop at the rental shop and pick up his tux, a three-car accident, while not serious, had tied up traffic, leaving him with a scant fifteen minutes to shower and change before leaving for the awards banquet.

"Sasha?" he called as he entered the apartment. "I'm sorry I'm late, but this damn hay truck got caught under a freeway underpass, then a guy in a pickup swerved to miss hitting the bales of hay that fell off, and—"

His words stuck in his throat and his jaw dropped as he caught sight of the stranger standing in his bedroom. "Sasha?"

The glamorous woman behind the makeup counter at Saks who had, at Margaret's prompting, sold Sasha enough cosmetics to open her own salon, had helpfully drawn the application instructions on the sketch of a face. Sasha had followed the instructions carefully, and after numerous failed attempts, thought she'd succeeded. But the way Mitch was staring at her—as if he'd never seen her before—made her worry that she'd overdone the makeover.

"Is something wrong?" It was the eyeliner! She'd known it was a mistake!

He opened his mouth to answer, but his stunned mind could not come up with the appropriate words. All he could do was shake his head.

He'd known she was pretty. Even, on occasion, beautiful, in a sweet, natural sort of way. But never in a million years could Mitch have imagined that Sasha could be so breathtakingly sexy.

The kohl liner made her smoldering eyes look even larger and darker than usual. A deep slash of color accented her chiseled Russian cheekbones, and her lips, glistening with gloss, made him think of ripe, succulent berries.

As for that skimpy excuse of a dress... it was both strangely innocent and outrageously alluring. As the dangling crystal earrings drew his attention to her bare shoulders, he felt a sudden, almost irresistible urge to sink his teeth into that gleaming skin.

"You do not like my new dress?" Her wet, ruby-red, eat-me-up mouth turned downward. Her hands ran over the sparkling scarlet fabric in an unconscious caress that made his mouth go dry. "I can change, if you'd like."

"No!" The word came out on an explosion of pent-up breath. "No," he repeated as his stomach muscles tightened into treacherous knots. "Don't change a thing. I was just surprised, that's all." He cleared his throat. "I wasn't expecting, I didn't know...aw, hell."

He dragged his hands through his hair as he continued to stare at her, wondering what, if anything, she was wearing beneath that sparkly, fire-engine-red, baby-doll dress.

It was working! Giddy with newfound feminine power, Sasha held out her arms and slowly turned on the dangerously spindly high heels. "Your sister picked it out."

"Remind me to thank her."

"I will do that." She smiled at him over her bare shoulder, a slow, seductive siren's smile that promised untold erotic delights. "Tomorrow morning." She glanced down her bare back at her legs. "Oh, dear," she sighed prettily, "I told Katie these stockings would prove a challenge."

The damn stockings in question had seams, Mitch realized, slender black ones that lured a guy's eyes all the way from her trim little ankles to where the dark lines disappeared beneath that scandalously short skirt. As she bent over to ostensibly straighten the right seam, blood rushed hotly from his head, flooding straight to his groin.

"Lord, lady." His deep voice was strained and husky with hunger.

"Is something wrong?" she asked innocently.

He shook his head. "Not a thing."

"I'm glad. This is your special night, Mitch. Everything should be perfect." Satisfied, she straightened. "How is that? Are they straight now?"

Knowing how a suicidal man felt when looking over the ledge atop a skyscraper, Mitch made himself take a longer look at those amazing legs. "Perfect." Lord, perfect didn't even begin to describe it.

He wanted to run his hands all the way up that glistening dark silk; he wanted to roll those stockings down, centimeter by centimeter, tasting each bit of warm ivory flesh. He wanted to lick her, bite her, eat her up. He wanted her in a way he'd never—ever—wanted a woman before.

He tossed the tux in its plastic bag onto the bed, then crossed the few feet separating them and ran his hands down her arms.

"Mrs. Cudahy, I do think you're trying to seduce me."

His eyes were dark and dangerous. Sasha was thrilled by the desire in those stormy blue depths. "Why, whatever made you think such a thing?" she asked with blatantly feigned innocence.

"Let's just say it was an educated guess." He smiled, enjoying the moment. "I have an idea."

"Last time you had an idea, I ended up getting married." She laughed and tossed her head, causing a frothy ebony cloud of hair to drift over her naked shoulders. "I'm almost afraid to ask what you've come up with this time."

The stunning metamorphosis went beyond the change in clothing and makeup, Mitch realized. Her entire personality had changed, as if someone had broken into the apartment while he'd been at the station, kidnapped his sweet, shy little bride and left this sexy vixen in her place.

"You really want to know what I've come up with?" He took her slender, beringed hand in his and pressed her palm against the front of his jeans. "How's this for starters?"

Beneath the denim barrier, he was hard as a boulder. And seemingly as large. Even as she feared she'd never be able to take all of him inside her, Sasha felt herself growing warm and wet between her thighs.

"That's a very good start." Obviously Katie had been right about her new outfit being dangerous ammunition. It appeared Mitch was more than ready to surrender the seduction battle. "But don't you think you should be getting ready to leave for your awards ceremony? As you said, you were late getting home and we don't have much time."

"How about we just stay home? Like an old married couple?"

"I would like that." She sighed dramatically, drawing attention to her perfumed breasts. "But unfortunately, it wouldn't be fair to disappoint so many people. After all, the dinner is in your honor. And it's for charity."

Her caressing fingers caused desire to pool and throb. If she kept it up, there would be no way he'd be able to walk into that ballroom without wearing his fireman's jacket to hide his aching arousal.

He lifted her treacherous hand to his lips and touched the tip of his tongue against the slender blue vein on the inside of her wrist. "I guess you're right." He looked at her over their linked fingers. "I suppose, if I were to kiss you, I'd mess up your lipstick."

"I think, Mitch," she said honestly, "that if you were to kiss me, we would never get to the banquet."

"True." His sigh was rougher and deeper than hers had been.

"I suppose it was unfair of me to wear such a revealing dress when you are trying so hard to be a gentleman." There was not a scintilla of apology in either her tone or her expression.

"A gentleman wouldn't be thinking the thoughts that flimsy excuse of a dress inspires. And I'll admit that I couldn't breathe when I first walked in the door and saw you wearing it. But it's more than that, Sasha.

"Whatever I'm feeling for you is a helluva lot more complicated than animal lust caused by a skimpy red dress and hooker heels." His gaze skimmed down her legs. "Although they are pretty terrific."

Despite the seriousness of the topic, Sasha laughed. "The shoes were your mother's contribution. I've been worrying all day that I won't be able to walk in them."

"Don't worry your gorgeous head about that little problem. I think it's my husbandly duty to hold you up."

He rocked forward on the balls of his feet, as if intending to kiss her on the mouth. At the last minute he changed course and touched his lips to her powdered cheek instead. "Since we have to go to this shindig, I'd better go shower and get dressed."

An unpalatable thought occurred to her. While she'd spent a long luxurious time bathing in the perfumed water, contemplating her seduction plans, she'd completely forgotten that Mitch would be needing a shower, as well. "I hope I left you enough hot water."

He laughed at that. "Darlin', that's the least of my worries."

He went into the bathroom and stripped off his clothes, trying to prevent ruining his chances for a future family while gingerly unzipping his too-tight jeans.

As he stepped beneath the purposefully icy water that did nothing to lessen his desire for his stunningly alluring wife, Mitch told himself that it was going to be a very long evening.

THE AWARDS DINNER was held in a resort ballroom overlooking formal gardens and a golf course. To Mitch's delight, amazement, and physical discomfort, Sasha tormented him all during dinner.

Under the long, white damask cloth covering the head table she slipped one foot out of her high-heeled shoe and ran her stocking-clad toes up his calf beneath his trouser leg, while her free hand stroked his thigh.

During dessert, while the introductory speaker droned on and on, she slanted him a coy glance from beneath the dark fringe of her lashes as she slowly, deliberately, licked a bit of whipped cream from her top lip. Watching her, Mitch felt his blood pressure soar through the high gilt ceiling.

"You realize," he murmured, his own hand delving beneath the tablecloth to squeeze her smooth leg, "that you're playing with fire."

"Ah, but you're a fireman, Mitch," she responded in a lush, silky voice he'd never heard from her before. "Surely you're capable of handling a few flames."

"I like to think so." His fingers were making slow, melting circles against the sensitive skin on the inside of her thighs. "The challenge is going to be, not to put the fire out too soon."

Before she could respond, Mitch realized that the speaker had finally called his name, drawing applause from the gathered crowd below the dais.

"Later," he murmured in Sasha's ear as he tossed his napkin onto the table and stood.

"Promises, promises," she murmured with a dangerous siren's smile that momentarily wiped his mind as clean as glass.

It took Mitch a moment to recover. Then, as he looked out over the audience and saw his mother and sister seated at a front table, he remembered what he'd wanted to say.

"I want to thank the governor, the mayor, and everyone on the citizens' council who voted me this honor," he said. "And it is an honor. But the truth is, I don't deserve it." Ignoring the unified intake of breath that rippled across the room, he continued. "At least no more than any of the other fire fighters—and cops—who put their lives on the line every day.

"People have this romantic notion that we fight fires and bad guys because of some strong inner urge to help people. And that's true. But most of all, we do it because there's nothing—well, almost nothing—" he amended, with a quick grin toward Sasha that caused a few chuckles "—that gives a greater high than the job.

"Thirty years ago my father received this same award for rescuing three of his fellow smoke eaters from a department store after the roof had fallen in on them."

He held the plaque in his hand and looked down at it, as if imagining that day. "I wasn't born yet, but I was lucky enough to witness many more acts of heroism. Such as the day he showed up at the ballpark, still sooty and drenched in sweat from fighting a desert grass fire, in time to watch me pitch in a Little League playoff game.

"Or when my sister Katie had an attack of appendicitis while we were camping and he drove like a maniac while assuring us all the way down from the mountains that she was going to be okay. And we knew she would be. Because Pops promised."

He paused again, his warm gaze sweeping over his mother—who surreptitiously wiped a tear away with the back of her finger—and his sister, who smiled back at him through moisture-bright eyes.

"Garrett Cudahy was a generous, faithful husband, a strict but loving father, and yes, a man who chose to fight fires as his life's work because he truly loved people.

"If I can ever become half the man my father was then, and only then, will I even begin to consider myself a hero. Like my pop."

He descended the few stairs to the floor to a standing ovation, handed the plaque to Margaret, kissed her on her wet cheek, accepted a kiss from Katie and a handshake from Jake, then returned to his seat.

"That was wonderful," Sasha said, her own eyes bright with tears. And then, because it had been too long since she'd kissed her husband, she brought his mouth to hers, causing another thunderous burst of applause.

"That reminds me," the governor said as he stood up again to officially end the awards portion of the evening. "It may come as a disappointment to any single ladies out there, but Mitch has recently gotten himself hitched." He smiled at Sasha, who'd reluctantly surrendered Mitch's lips. "Cudahy, you are not only a hero, you are a very lucky man."

There was more laughter. Then, on cue, the band began playing, inviting couples onto the dance floor.

When Mitch held out his hand to Sasha, she didn't hesitate. And when he gathered her into his arms and they began swaying slowly to the music, she knew that she'd never been happier.

"That was a very nice thing to do," she murmured. "Talking about your father like that."

"It was true." Mitch pressed his lips against the top of her head. "Pops was the best." He trailed his hand down her back and, unable to resist the lure of all that creamy bare skin, bent his head and kissed her neck, her shoulder.

Sasha sighed and closed her eyes as she allowed her own hands to play in his hair.

"I wish I could have met him."

"You would have liked him." He pulled her closer, enjoying the feel of her soft breasts pressed against his chest. As her smooth thighs brushed against his legs, he felt a resurgence of the desire he'd managed, just barely, to bank long enough to give his brief acceptance speech. "And he would have liked you."

It was the truth. Although at first he'd mistakenly considered Sasha a victim—a poor little Russian waif in need of rescuing—he'd come to realize that the lady had a helluva lot of guts to leave her country and the only life she'd ever known, to cross an ocean, seeking a father who could turn out to be nothing but a fanciful story told by a mother who wanted her daughter to grow up believing she'd been conceived in love.

Sasha opened her eyes and tilted her head back to look up at him. "Do you really think so?"

"Absolutely." He smiled and brushed the back of his hand up the side of her face, pleased by the soft drift of pale pink color that bloomed beneath his caressing touch. "He'd say you had gumption."

She sighed her pleasure, wondering what it would do to Mitch's heroic reputation to have his wife melt into a little puddle of need right in the middle of a public dance floor.

"This is good? This gumption?"

"The best."

She thought about that, and smiled. "Mitch?"

"Mmm?" He gave her earlobe a playful nip.

A mist of arousal was drifting over her mind, wrapping her in a silvery haze of pleasure. "Did it upset you? When the governor told everyone you were married?"

Mitch smiled, amazed by the change Sasha had wrought in his life in such a short time. "Actually, if you want to know the absolute truth, I was proud."

"Really?"

Looking down into her exquisite face, Mitch felt the hunger he always experienced when he was around Sasha meld with an easy affection he had never expected to feel for her.

"Really. Watching every male in the room lusting after a woman and knowing she's going home with you arouses some very primal feelings."

"Primal?" She smiled up at him. "Although your English is admittedly better than mine, Mitch, I believe the word you are looking for is possessive."

Mitch grinned. Enjoying the evening. Enjoying her. "Guilty." He cupped her chin between his fingers and bent his head. His lips hovered a breath above hers, nearly close enough for tasting. "How would you like to take a little stroll out on the golf course with your husband?"

Smiling, she touched the tip of her tongue against her top lip. Then, daringly, against his. "I thought you would never ask."

A full moon rode in a clear desert sky, shining its soft silver light over the velvety dark lawn. The perfume of bougainvillaea, hibiscus and roses drifted on the warm air from the nearby gardens. Fingers linked, Mitch pulled Sasha away from the ballroom terrace, across the greens, into a grove of pyramid-shaped silk oak trees.

"Alone at last," he breathed, then lowered his mouth to hers.

Sasha had expected passion. And fire. And lightning. Instead, she was being treated to a pleasure so sweet, so sublime, it nearly made her weep. Images tumbled seductively through her mind—flickering yellow candlelight, lush red roses, she and Mitch entwined on white satin sheets.

Even as his strong hands played in her hair, she longed for them to touch her everywhere. Even as his firm lips plucked enticingly at hers, drawing her deeper and deeper into a warm, fluid passion, she wished to feel his mouth against every inch of her heated flesh.

Although urgency rose, Mitch kept the pace slow, pleasuring himself, pleasuring her. His lips took a leisurely journey over her face, brushing heat against her temples, before moving on to her closed lids.

"You're trembling," he murmured as he tasted the fragrant flesh behind her ear.

"I know." His warm breath, his tender kisses, were making her knees weak. "I can't help it."

He pulled back and smiled into her eyes. Those wide, wonderful, expressive eyes. "Believe me, darlin', I know the feeling." Still smiling, he slowly and deliberately took her mouth again.

Tension twisted in his gut as he deepened the kiss, degree by devastating degree. Mitch had kissed more women than he could count, but never had a mere kiss made him ache. And never had kissing any other woman made him tremble.

She was so sweet. So soft. And she was his!

As Mitch reveled in that thought, the part of his brain that was still functioning rationally took note of a distant, familiar sound.

"Aw, hell," he groaned just as the golf course sprinklers turned on, shooting a fountain of water into the air, drenching them both.

13

"OH, NO!" Sasha shrieked. And then let loose with a torrent of passionate Russian.

"I suppose we could have used some cooling off," he admitted, raining short, laughing kisses over her wet face. "But this is ridiculous."

She was laughing, as well, as she kissed him back. "No matter what Ben Houston said, I do not think I am your good luck charm, Mitch. In fact, I am beginning to worry that I bring you bad luck."

"Never." He stopped laughing long enough to frame her face between his palms and hold her smiling gaze to his. "Although I was too dense to realize it at the time, Sasha Mikhailova Cudahy, I'm beginning to think the day we got married may just have been the luckiest day of my life."

Oblivious to the water streaming over them, soaking her carefully created hairstyle, melting the makeup she'd spent so much time on, ruining her new, ridiculously expensive dress, Sasha was suddenly frozen to the spot. Her wide eyes, still laced with lingering desire and laughter, swept over his handsome face, studying him intently.

"I believe you mean that," she said finally.

"You believe right." He traced her parted lips with his thumb, remembering their taste, and imagined what they would feel like skimming their way all over his naked body. "And although I've tried to play by the rules of our agreement, sometime between when I walked into the bedroom and saw you looking like every male's midnight fantasy and when those damn sprinklers went off, I realized that I can't do it.

"I want to make mad, passionate love to my wife."

She flung her arms around his neck and clung to him. "Oh, yes!"

LATER, WHEN SHE TRIED to recreate the evening, wanting to tuck every golden moment of it away in her mind the way a teenage girl might save an orchid prom corsage or a bride might preserve her lace-and-satin wedding dress, Sasha would realize that she had absolutely no memory of leaving the resort and driving back home to Mitch's apartment.

But somehow they must have managed it, because the next thing she knew, he was scooping her up into his arms, the same wonderful way he had in the casino, and was carrying her through the front door.

"I only had one glass of wine with dinner," she said, afraid he might think her uncharacteristically sexy behavior was due to too much alcohol. "I am not drunk. Like in Laughlin."

"I know." He looked down into her soft, lovely face and saw not the ruined makeup she'd so painstakingly applied, but her tenderness, her love.

My woman. The thought ricocheted through his mind as he kicked the door shut behind him, managing somehow to latch the chain lock. "But it's an old American tradition for a groom to carry his bride across the threshold."

He kissed her, a long, deep, moist kiss that left her head spinning even more than it had after all the champagne in the casino.

"I think I like this tradition," she managed when the blissful kiss ended. "Very much."

"You and me both, darlin'." Taking her mouth again, he carried her into the bedroom. They fell on the bed together, rolling over the mattress, arms and legs tangled, hands lighting flames on anxious bodies that had waited too long for fulfillment.

"I have dreamed of this," she managed, her mouth feasting on his as hungrily as he was eating into hers.

Even as she confessed her erotic secret, Sasha knew that it wasn't the same. Because as thrilling as those sensual dreams had been, they didn't come close to this aching reality.

Somehow, Mitch managed to yank the wet dress over her head without tearing it, then, with greedy hands ripped the brief strapless bra away as well. When he took her breast in his mouth, a surge of fire shot through Sasha like a flaming brand. The wooden bed frame groaned as she bucked upward, raking her hands in his hair, pressing him deeper into her burning, yielding flesh.

She cried out in wonder when Mitch's teeth captured a rigid tip, biting down in a way that sent the first wave crashing through her. Desperate to touch him as he was touching her, she tugged his shirt out of his slacks and began fumbling with the front of his pleated and starched shirtfront.

"I can't..." Her voice trembling, she swore in Russian when it looked as if the unfamiliar jet studs were going to defeat her.

"Here." The single word exploded on a torment of shared frustration. "Let me." Heedless of the rental cost, Mitch tore the shirt open, sending studs flying across the room. Then he pulled her against him, crushing her breasts against his chest, their mouths feeding ravenously again as they rolled over the bed, kicking off shoes, ripping at clothes, demanding, offering, taking.

Pillows tumbled to the carpet and went unnoticed. Mitch swore as they tangled in the bedspread, managed to rip it from beneath her and throw it in the direction of a nearby chair.

Here was the fire he'd warned her about playing with earlier. The glorious conflagration she'd been longing to experience. His hard, taut body was like a furnace, the flames licking higher and higher, and he pressed her deeper and deeper into the mattress, making her glow from the inside out. His mouth burned into hers, sending tongues of flame flickering across her damp flesh, heating her degree by treacherous degree.

My woman. The refrain repeated over and over again in his mind, like a bridge from a never sung yet strangely familiar song. Mitch had promised himself that he'd be gentle; had vowed to be tender. But as the waves of fire scorched through his mind and the billowing smoke blinded him, for the first time in his life he felt the need to conquer. To possess. To claim his bride for his own, for all time.

The heat was unbearable. When he pressed his palm against that secret place between her legs where damp warmth flowed, she gathered up handfuls of crumpled sheet.

"Oh, please," she gasped as his mouth replaced his hand, sending white-hot flames licking through her blood. Another wave of ecstasy swept outward from that ultrasensitive core like wildfire, leaving her gasping and panting. And, unbelievably, wanting more.

"I need you, Mitch." If begging was what was necessary to end this torment, Sasha would beg. She would crawl. Or scream. Whatever it took. She couldn't wait any longer.

Calling out his name, she dragged his mouth back to her hot avid one and wrapped her legs around his hips in a viselike grip. "I need you," she repeated raggedly. "Now."

Filled with a fierceness that frightened him, Mitch braced himself on his elbows and looked down at her, his blue eyes dark and savage. "Sweet heaven, I need you, too." He moved his hips forward, pressing against her, rekindling hot glowing coals that he had no intention of allowing to cool. "And that scares the hell out of me."

Before she could answer, before she could tell him that the enormity of her love for him was frightening to her, as well, he plunged into her with a force just this side of violence. Her body shuddered as he broke through the virginal barrier, taking her innocence while bringing her a pleasure that overwhelmed any fleeting pain. Loving him as she'd never dreamed of loving any man, Sasha twined her arms around his neck and opened for him—lips, mind, body, heart.

It was like being enveloped in molten satin. Hot and smooth and unbearably erotic. Mitch began to move, slowly at first, then faster, his strokes harder, deeper as he drove her, drove them both, into the inferno.

She cried out his name on a gasp of pleasure an instant before his own ragged shout tore from his burning throat.

My wife. With that last coherent thought, Mitch flooded into her.

They lay together, arms and legs entwined, Mitch's mouth buried into the fragrant flesh of her neck, enjoying the soothing afterglow of passion. As impossible as it seemed, every nerve ending in Sasha's body was still tingling, making her feel more alive than she'd ever felt in her life.

"I'm sorry." His words vibrated against her damp skin.

"Sorry?" The odd tone in his voice made her look up at him with curiosity. "What could you possibly be sorry about?"

"You were a virgin." He'd known that, but his need for her had scorched the knowledge from his mind.

"Yes. But surely you knew that."

"Of course I did. Which is why I should have taken you with more finesse."

Finesse. Such a pretty word. Such a polite, civilized word. For something that had been in no way even remotely civilized.

"I think it was perfect. Just the way it was." She took his hand in hers and pressed it against her still-pulsating body. "Feel what you have done."

Inner eruptions exploded against his palm. "I did that?"

"I do not see anyone else in this bed." She was bathed in a golden glow that made her smile. "That was the most special thing that has ever happened to me."

He combed his fingers idly through the dark curls between her thighs, loving the way her jet pupils were already expanding with renewed desire.

"To me, too." Although her body's instinctively sensual response to his stroking touch was making him hard again, Mitch was afraid that to take her again, so soon, might cause her pain. So he managed, just barely, to restrain himself. For now.

He ran his hand down her side, from her breasts to her thighs. "Did I mention that I love those stockings?"

"Not in words."

She cuddled against him, thinking that as wondrous as his lovemaking had been, this settling down, talking period afterward was nearly as enjoyable.

"But I could tell you found them appealing," she said, feeling that delicious desire building all over again.

"What was your first clue?" He toyed with the elastic band holding them up. "The fact that I looked as if I was on the verge of exploding when you pulled that seam-straightening stunt."

She giggled softly. "I suppose that was unfair. But I wanted you to think of me as a sexy woman."

"If that was your intention, sweetheart, it sure worked."
He slipped his fingers between the stocking and her warm
flesh. "But it was also unnecessary, since I'd already decided that you were pretty damn sexy the first time I saw you
in that bubblegum-pink uniform."

She laughed again, a soft shimmer of sound that slipped
silkily into his blood. "That was such an ugly dress."

He wasn't going to argue the point. It was, after all, true.
"Which is why it's so amazing you could look so good in
it." He smoothed the stocking back up her thigh with both
hands, then sat back on his haunches, enjoying the contrast between her smooth ivory thighs and those long dark
stockings.

"How did you manage to wear these with that short skirt,
anyway?"

"Katie taught me a trick." She was totally vulnerable, lying there, naked, her legs spread, open to his gaze. She
would have expected to feel embarrassed, but as his fingers
trailed seductive little circles on the sensitive flesh on the
inside of her thighs, she experienced instead feminine pride
that her husband would find her so appealing.

"She said that if I bought the larger size..." His stroking touch was causing renewed desire to pool inside her. "If
I bought the larger size they would go up higher on my leg...
Mitch!" She began to tremble as he touched his lips against
that still-tingling flesh. "How do you expect me to answer
you if you keep distracting me?"

"Sorry." His rakish grin, as he looked up at her, said just
the opposite. "Am I a distraction?"

"You know you are."

"Serves you right." When his teeth nipped at that ultrasensitive nub, a ragged moan slipped from between her ravished lips. "After the way you tried to seduce me."

"I did not try." She grabbed him by the hair and lifted his head again and gave him a blatantly female, unmistakably satisfied look. "I succeeded."

He laughed, as he was meant to. "Touché." He rocked forward and brushed his mouth against hers. Sweetly. Tenderly. As if they had all the time in the world. "There's an old American saying," he murmured. "What's sauce for the goose is sauce for the gander."

"I do not think I know that one."

"It means—" his fingers slipped smoothly into her slick heat "—I think it's only fair that this time I seduce you."

Her lips curved beneath his. "I am so happy that I married such a fair-minded man."

Twining her arms around his neck, Sasha invited her husband to take her back into the mists.

Which he did. Again and again. All night long.

WHILE MITCH MANAGED to catch some much needed sleep, Sasha crept quietly into the kitchen, determined make him a proper American breakfast. "What could be more American than waffles?" she asked herself as she took the box from the freezer.

There was just one little problem. She'd ruined the toaster last week by filling it with foam. Never one to let small obstacles defeat her, she turned on the oven and put the frozen squares onto a cookie sheet.

She'd just put the cookie sheet on the oven rack when the phone rang. Before she could answer it, she heard Mitch's voice coming from the bedroom.

"Yeah?" he grumbled, irritated by having been roused out of a dream where he was making love to Sasha beneath a waterfall.

"Mitch? Did I wake you?"

Mitch tensed at the familiar voice. "Actually, you did."
He glanced up at Sasha, who was standing in the bedroom
doorway, clad in a froth of silk and ivory lace, looking
downright delectable.

"This isn't a real good time." When she entered the bedroom, a beam of sunlight rendered the sheer gown nearly
invisible. Mitch sucked in a sharp breath. "How about I call
you back later?"

"Actually, I wanted to talk with Sasha, anyway."

"What about?" Mitch asked suspiciously.

Meredith laughed at that, a low, sultry laugh that didn't
affect him nearly as much as Sasha's light, musical one.
"Don't worry, darling, I'm not going to share female war
stories with your bride. I just want to talk to her about our
interview."

"Interview? What interview?"

"Oh, dear. I take it you don't know." She paused. "Well,
if your wife hasn't discussed it with you, I'm certainly not
going to say a thing. Could you just put her on the phone?"

He held the receiver toward Sasha. "It's Meredith Roberts. Something about an interview."

"Oh, yes!" She took the phone and sat down on the edge
of the bed. "Hello, Meredith. Your station is running it?"

"Monday and Tuesday nights. In segments at six and ten
o'clock."

"That is very good news! I appreciate this very much,
Meredith."

"I told you, it's a good story. The kind of touchy feely
thing people want. Thanks for giving me the exclusive." Her
message delivered, the reporter hung up.

"I didn't know you'd given Meredith an interview,"
Mitch said.

"I was going to tell you—" Sasha handed him back the
receiver "—but I didn't know if the station would run the

story, so I waited. Besides, you were at work so much last week, and I was at the school, and then I made the decision to tell you after the banquet, but—''

''Afterward, I was distracted.''

''Yes.'' Sasha watched the desire rise in his eyes and felt a similar heat begin to glow inside her. ''Meredith says there's a chance the networks might pick up my story.''

''That could be a help.'' He ran his hand down her tousled hair, over her bare shoulders. ''Maybe someone will see it who knows your father.''

''That's what Meredith said,'' she agreed breathlessly as his caressing touch made her feel as if she was going to melt.

It was amazing. Mitch had thought his obsession for this woman was born of sexual frustration. But he'd taken care of that little problem last night. And each time they'd made love, he'd been left wanting more. As he still did this morning.

''I missed you,'' he said, pulling her against him.

''You were sleeping.''

''Ah, but I knew you weren't beside me. Where you belonged.''

He touched his mouth to her silky skin. ''I take it this is one of your shower presents?''

''Yes. Do you like it?''

''Sweetheart, like doesn't even begin to come close.'' He untied the satin ribbon lacing the front of the gown together. ''It's just too bad I'm going to have to take it off you.''

As he nuzzled his face between her silky breasts, Sasha combed her hands though his thick hair and fell back against the pillows as that delicious, enervating heat began to spread through her bloodstream.

''You're making my head spin,'' she complained on a long, shuddering sigh.

"Good." He cut a wet swath up her throat to her mouth with his tongue. "Let's see if we can make the rest of you spin."

Of course, he could. And, in turn, Sasha did the same to him. Bathed in the benevolent golden glow of a desert morning, they spent a long leisurely time pleasuring each other, pledging vows with words and bodies and hearts. And it was glorious.

He could spend the rest of his life right here, Mitch decided much, much later as he lay steeped in this woman who'd come to mean so much to him in so short a time. She was lying in his arms, her head nestled against his shoulder. From her slow, soft breathing, he realized she'd fallen asleep.

He could use some more sleep, as well. But his mind wouldn't rest. It was too filled with Sasha—her scent, her feel, her taste.

Mitch had never been much for introspection. He'd always lived for the moment, which for the first twenty-seven years of his life, had suited him just fine. But now he realized that falling in love was even more dangerous—and more exhilarating—than running into a burning building.

He pressed his lips against her hair. When she smiled, and stirred and wrapped her arms tighter around him, he felt a sense of rightness he'd never felt before. Closing his eyes, he drifted back to sleep.

MITCH WAS AWAKENED by a siren's blare echoing through the room. He was out of the bed like a shot, reaching automatically for the clothes he always kept within arm's reach, and cursed when they weren't there.

"Oh, no!" As he watched Sasha leap from the bed and go racing into the kitchen, Mitch's first thought was to wonder what his wife—his naked wife!—was doing at the station. A second later, comprehension dawned and he realized where he was. And what was making that godawful air raid sound.

Following her into the kitchen, he waded through the billowing gray smoke and watched as she pulled a cookie sheet from the oven.

"Am I allowed to ask what those were?" he inquired as she threw the black squares into the sink and proceeded to drown them beneath the faucet. He reached up and reset the smoke detector, silencing it.

"I'm sorry! I wanted to make you a nice breakfast, like a good American wife..."

"That was breakfast?"

"Waffles." She shook her head. "I'm such a failure!"

"So you can't cook." He crossed the room and gathered her into his arms, gently tilting her chin up to meet his reassuring gaze. "You can learn. Or I can learn. Or we both can." He traced her quivering lips with his thumb. "Or we can eat all our meals out." He touched his mouth to hers. "Or, better yet, live on love."

"We would waste away."

He pulled her even closer and deepened the kiss, literally stealing her breath. "But what a way to go," he said when they finally came up for air.

Reluctantly he released her, and began opening windows.

14

AFTER THEY'D FINISHED the breakfast Mitch picked up for them at Glory's, he suggested spending the night at a French country inn in Sedona.

Sasha found the magnificent red rock country of Oak Creek Canyon awe-inspiring. "I can't remember ever being so relaxed. Or so happy."

"Neither can I." They were sitting on a wrought-iron bench beneath the spreading green canopy of an oak tree.

They'd spent the Sunday drive up from Phoenix talking. Mitch had told Sasha things he'd never told any other person—not even his mother, whom he dearly loved.

He admitted the pain and debilitating sense of loss he'd experienced in those days following the fire that had taken his father's life and how he'd felt he could never live up to Garrett Cudahy's hero image. And how he believed that his father still watched over him, and hopefully approved of how he'd chosen to live his own life.

In turn, Sasha shared much of her life with him—a hard life filled with struggles and loneliness, which confirmed what he'd already figured out for himself.

And now, as they sat beside the crystal stream, she told him stories her mother had told her, romanticized tales of how their life would be when they reached America.

"My father was going to buy a house with many flowers. And a wide, covered front porch with a swing. The house would be blue with white shutters. And there would be clay pots overflowing with bright red geraniums on the porch." She smiled. "Mama always called it their red, white and blue American house."

"It sounds nice."

"Yes," she sighed, "it does."

Hearing the faint sadness creeping back into her tone, Mitch caught her downcast chin in his fingers and turned her head toward him. "We'll find him," he promised.

Mitch was a hero. Her hero. But he was not a miracle worker. After a year of failure after failure, Sasha no longer held out a great deal of hope. But not wanting to ruin this exquisite afternoon, she reminded herself how lucky she was to have found such a kind and loving man.

"Yes." She wrapped her arms around him, tight. "Mitch?"

"Mmm?" He buried his lips in her hair and breathed in her light, flowery scent.

"I am suddenly very tired. Do you think we have time for a short nap before dinner?"

"Darlin'—" he stood and lifted her into his arms "—I'm suddenly overcome with an attack of exhaustion myself."

Laughing, Sasha pressed her lips to his as he carried her back across the lawn to their cottage.

THE INTERVIEW AIRED, as promised, on Monday and Tuesday of the following week. It was also, Sasha had been excited to learn, picked up by the network.

On Wednesday morning, a woman in a taupe suit and carrying a briefcase arrived at the apartment door.

"Mrs. Cudahy?" She greeted Sasha with a friendly smile.

"Yes. I am Mrs. Cudahy." Sasha thought it both strange and wonderful how she'd grown accustomed to answering to Mitch's last name.

"I'm Mrs. Kensington. From the U.S. Immigration Service. May I come in?"

"Of course!" Sasha stepped aside, glancing past the woman, half expecting to see her nemesis lurking nearby.

"I've been assigned your case, Mrs. Cudahy," the woman said, answering Sasha's unspoken question.

Mitch chose that moment to wander in from the bedroom, clad in jeans and bare feet. He was buttoning a blue chambray shirt. "What happened to the weasel?" The possessive way he put his arm around Sasha's too-rigid shoulders did not escape the immigration officer's professionally trained eyes.

"I assume you're referring to Mr. Potter." A hint of a smile tugged at her lips. "He was reassigned yesterday."

"Reassigned?" Sasha asked.

"Actually, I believe a more accurate word is demoted." The satisfaction in the woman's eyes suggested to Mitch that Potter had made life as uncomfortable for his fellow workers as for Sasha and all the other poor immigrants unlucky enough to have him assigned to their cases. "Our regional director was not exactly pleased with how your network interview made our office look."

As he felt Sasha begin to relax, Mitch decided to send Meredith a dozen roses for having solved one of Sasha's problems so neatly.

"So," he said, squeezing Sasha's shoulder reassuringly, "I suppose you're here for the home visit."

"Yes." The woman glanced down at her watch. "But since my caseload has more than doubled since inheriting Mr. Potter's files, I'd better be on my way."

"That's it?" Even Mitch was surprised.

"That's it," the woman agreed.

"Did we pass?" Sasha risked asking.

"With flying colors." She glanced at the two cups and two cereal bowls still on the kitchen table. "It's obvious you're living as man and wife. It's also obvious that you care for one another. And, after such a remarkably sympathetic network appearance relating your attempts to locate your father, we'd look like Scrooge if we tried to deport you," she assured Sasha with a warm smile.

"It will take a few weeks for the paperwork to clear." She held out her hand. "In the meantime, welcome to America."

As she shook the woman's hand, Sasha felt the tears begin to overflow. But this time they were tears of joy.

TWO DAYS LATER, after Mitch had left for the station, Meredith telephoned.

"I just received a call," the reporter said. "From your father. He wants to meet you."

"Really?" Although Sasha's suddenly frantically beating heart wanted to believe that this was the happy ending she'd been searching for, her head reminded her of all the other times she'd been disappointed.

"Really. Actually, he wants you to come live with him."

"Live with him?"

"In Big Sur. South of San Francisco. Seems he's got a huge house—one of those glass and redwood things—overlooking the beach. Looks as if you struck it rich, Sasha.

"Of course we'll want to film your reunion. It'll make a dynamite Cinderella story—how the penniless little immigrant waif discovers the streets in America really are paved with gold."

The knowledge that her father wanted her after all these years, should have given Sasha pleasure. Instead she felt a shadow move over her heart. Her mind went numb as she wrote down the information.

MITCH WAS GLAD when the day turned out to be one emergency after another. It kept him from thinking of Sasha. Of how much he missed her.

He was grinning as the truck headed back to the station after putting out a car fire. For the first time, he understood why Jake had traded his sportscar for a minivan. There wasn't anything he wouldn't do for Sasha. Because somehow, when he wasn't looking, he'd fallen in love with his wife.

With that amazing, yet highly satisfying thought in his mind, Mitch idly glanced around at the neighborhood they were passing through. It was an older neighborhood, the kind with deep front lawns and mature trees, and small, but well-built houses sporting wide front porches that harkened back to days when an evening's entertainment meant sitting outside with a glass of ice-cold lemonade, watching your neighbors.

"Hey!" he shouted, pounding on the side of the truck. "Tell Jake to stop!"

The word filtered forward, fireman to fireman, to the cab of the truck where Jake was behind the wheel. He pulled over to the curb and leaned out the driver's window. "What's wrong?"

"I gotta check on something," Mitch said. "I'll be right back." He jogged back down the street to the information box attached to a white wooden For Sale sign surrounded by bright flowers.

This was it! Sasha's dream house. Right down to the blue siding, bright white shutters and the swing. All right, perhaps the red flowers were petunias instead of geraniums, but with that single exception, it could have been drawn straight from her mother's description.

He plucked a brochure from the box, tucked it into his jacket and returned to the truck.

"Thinking of doing a little nest building?" Jake asked with a knowing grin.

"Just drive," Mitch said, his own grin taking the edge off his words. "I want to get back to the station. I have a call to make."

He looked back at the house and pictured Sasha standing on the front steps, looking pert and sexy in her white nurse's uniform, welcoming him home with open arms while their baby slept in an old-fashioned blue buggy on the old-fashioned shaded porch.

The idea was more than a little appealing.

After talking with the real estate agent on the phone, Mitch was even more enthusiastic. The house sounded perfect. And what's more, he'd socked away enough to easily make the down payment.

Next on his agenda was to see the inside and make an offer before the house was snatched up.

"Hey, Jake," he asked his brother-in-law, whose three-day shift was just ending. "How'd you like to do me a big favor?"

"Like stick around while you take your bride to see her new home?"

One thing about so many guys living so close together was that privacy became a rare commodity. Mitch grinned. "Yeah."

Jake grinned back. "Since Katie would kill me if I screwed up a chance to make Sasha happy, it doesn't look as if I have much choice. So go play real estate magnate. And have fun."

"Thanks." Needing to wash the lingering smell of smoke from his hair, Mitch took a quick shower. When he came out of the communal bathroom, there were hoots of amusement.

"Nice undies, Mitchie," one of the firemen called out.

"Pink is definitely your color," another one pitched in.

"This is what marriage does to a guy," a third drawled. "Softens him up. Next thing you know, he'll be measuring the station windows for gingham curtains."

Mitch flashed them a good-natured middle finger and proceeded to finish dressing. So what if Sasha had messed up the wash? So what if she couldn't cook? He loved her. Just the way she was.

He was just about to call her, to tell her he was on the way home to pick her up for a surprise, when Jake called out, "Sasha's on the phone."

He took the receiver. "Hi, darlin'. Your timing's perfect. I was just getting ready to call you."

"I heard from my father," Sasha blurted out.

"What?" Mitch shook his head, certain he must have misunderstood her.

"I said, my father called me. Just a few minutes ago."

He still didn't understand. "How—"

"He saw Meredith's report on the network broadcast and called her. She gave him my number."

"I see." Wondering how this was going to affect their marriage, Mitch paused and let out a long breath. "Well, this is what you've been wanting."

"Yes." She did not sound all that enthusiastic.

"So. How did it go?"

"Very well, actually." It was her turn to let out a breath. "He wants me to come live with him, Mitch. In Big Sur."

Mitch waited for her to say that of course she'd told him that was impossible. That she already had a home—and a life—in Phoenix, with her husband.

Nothing. Just dead air coming from the other end of the telephone line.

"Big Sur, huh? Sounds like he's done okay for himself."

"He wrote a book on journalism that's required reading in most colleges. And some novels. Meredith said he's very rich."

"Looks as if you've hit the jackpot."

"That's what Meredith said."

The pause this time was longer. And deadlier.

"Congratulations," Mitch said finally. "I hope he's everything you wanted him to be. Look, Sasha, I'd love to talk some more, but I've got a fire to go to."

He hung up before he resorted to begging. Then slammed his fist into the wall.

SITTING on the edge of the bed, Sasha stared down at the telephone receiver. He'd hung up on her. Just like that. And she knew he was lying. If there'd been a fire, she would have heard the alarm.

She'd done everything but beg him to ask her to stay. Couldn't he tell she didn't want to leave him to run off to Big Sur? Didn't he know how much she loved him? As she raised her hand to replace the receiver, the flash of her gold wedding band drew her attention to her reflection in the dresser mirror.

They were married. In front of Elvis they had promised to love and honor each other, for better or worse, for richer or poorer, in sickness and in health—forever. And although the marriage may have been fraudulent in the beginning, Mitch himself had pointed out that the rules had changed.

She was his wife. Mitch was her husband. That being the case, she wasn't going anywhere.

Except, Sasha amended, to the store. To buy a cookbook.

MITCH WAS LYING on his back on his bunk staring up at the ceiling. Although he knew how badly Sasha wanted to find her father, he also knew damn well that she loved him. And he loved her. That being the case, they belonged together. Forever.

They were married. And, if he had anything to say about it, they were going to stay married. "Hey, Jake..."

"I figured you'd change your mind," his brother-in-law drawled. "That's why I stuck around."

Before Mitch could thank him, the alarm blasted through the building. "Hey, Mitch," the dispatcher called out, "it's your apartment complex."

He cursed. Sasha must have been in the kitchen again. At least, he thought as he climbed onto the back of the truck, she hadn't been packing.

Mitch's mild irritation turned to terror when the truck rounded the corner and he could see that the building was engulfed in flames. Two other trucks from nearby stations had already arrived on the scene and the firemen were busy pouring water on the raging inferno.

"What the hell happened?" Mitch asked, grabbing the arm of the first fireman he saw.

"Nobody knows for sure." The man pointed the stream of water directly at Mitch's apartment. "But one of the neighbors says there's a kid living in the end apartment who thinks he's Mr. Wizard. Always fooling around with chemicals and stuff. He could have made a bad mix."

Mitch knew the kid. He should. His parents were his next-door neighbors. "What about the people inside?"

"Everyone's accounted for except some woman in the apartment next to the end one." The fireman raised his voice to be heard over the roar of the fire as it ate away a section of wooden roof shakes. "It's too hot to get up there and see."

His apartment! Mitch watched horrified as an explosion blew out the arcadia doors leading to his balcony. This time there was no way up the outside stairway. However, if he could make it to the roof of the adjoining units . . .

"Don't even think it," a voice shouted in his ear. Mitch turned and glared at Jake, who, officially off duty, had followed in his minivan.

"Sasha could be in there!"

"And she might not be," Jake said. "And I'm not about to explain to a pretty young bride that I let her husband kill himself with some damn fool stunt."

"She's my wife, dammit." When Jake grabbed his jacket, he reacted on instinct and swung.

Jake dodged the fist. "Sorry, hotshot." He landed a blow on Mitch's jaw, sending him sprawling into a pile of fire hoses.

That was how Sasha found them, rolling on the wet ground, arms flailing, fists flying, while all around them the firemen continued to fight the blaze, ignoring the fact that two of their own were engaged in a brawl.

"Mitch! Jake!" She dropped the plastic book bag, ran over to them, and began pulling them apart. "What are you doing?"

Adrenaline was pumping through Mitch's blood and fear had its icy grip on his mind, distorting his thinking process. It took him a minute to figure out that it was really Sasha who'd thrown herself on his back and was trying to grab hold of his hands.

"Mitch!" she shouted in his ear. "You must stop this! Now!"

"Yeah, Mitch!" Jake yelled. "Knock it off!"

Realization finally sank in. Mitch twisted around and stared up at her. "Sasha? You're safe?"

"Yes." She pressed a kiss against his mouth. "I am safe."

The breath went out of him in a deep, relieved whoosh. "I was so worried."

"I am sorry." She glanced up at the building that was engulfed in a cloud of steam as the fire hoses doused the flames. "I promise, Mitch. I was not cooking."

Her expression was so earnest, Mitch had to laugh. "Sweetheart, I wouldn't care if you had started it. So long as you're safe, that's all that matters."

Jake pushed himself to his feet. "Since you two lovebirds don't need any company, I think I'll go see about getting some ice for my eye. You pack one helluva punch."

"Sorry about that," Mitch said, not bothering to point out that Jake had gotten a few good licks of his own in.

"Hey, you were worried about your bride." Jake shrugged. "I would've behaved the same way if I'd thought Katie was up there."

When he was gone, Mitch said, "We need to talk."

Sasha nodded, and opened her mouth to respond when a sudden burst of water from a misdirected fire hose sent them skidding across the lawn. When they came to a stop, Mitch was lying on top of her. And they were both laughing.

"How come I always end up getting wet when I'm with you?"

"You're not the only one," she mused, grinning up at him.

"True." He tenderly pushed strands of wet hair away from her face and said, "I love you. And I don't want you to go to Big Sur."

His heart plummeted as tears flooded into her eyes. "I mean, to live," he said quickly. "Of course you want to visit your dad. But I want you to stay here with me."

"Oh, Mitch, I love you, too. And I wasn't going to leave you. Ever! You're stuck with me. For better or worse."

The way she was looking up at him made Mitch feel ten feet tall. He also decided that perhaps it wasn't so bad being a hero after all. As long as he could always be Sasha's hero.

"I found your house, Sasha. Your dream house. It's ours if we—you—want it."

Sasha stared up at him. It was too much. Her father, a husband, her American citizenship, and her dream house. *Their* dream house, she reminded herself. Hers and Mitch's. All in one glorious day!

Surely no woman had ever been luckier. Or happier. She laughed as she threw her arms around her husband. "My hero."

Harlequin Romance ®

Delightful

Affectionate

Romantic

Emotional

Tender

Original

Daring

Riveting

Enchanting

Adventurous

Moving

Harlequin Romance—the
series that has it all!

HROM-G

HARLEQUIN PRESENTS

HARLEQUIN PRESENTS
men you won't be able to resist falling in love with...

HARLEQUIN PRESENTS
women who have feelings just like your own...

HARLEQUIN PRESENTS
powerful passion in exotic international settings...

HARLEQUIN PRESENTS
intense, dramatic stories that will keep you turning
to the very last page...

HARLEQUIN PRESENTS
The world's bestselling romance series!

Harlequin® Historical

If you're a serious fan of historical romance,
then you're in luck!

Harlequin Historicals brings you
stories by bestselling authors, rising new stars
and talented first-timers.

Ruth Langan & Theresa Michaels
Mary McBride & Cheryl St.John
Margaret Moore & Merline Lovelace
Julie Tetel & Nina Beaumont
Susan Amarillas & Ana Seymour
Deborah Simmons & Linda Castle
Cassandra Austin & Emily French
Miranda Jarrett & Suzanne Barclay
DeLoras Scott & Laurie Grant...

You'll never run out of favorites.

Harlequin Historicals...they're too good to miss!

HH-GEN

LOOK FOR OUR FOUR FABULOUS MEN!

Each month some of today's bestselling authors bring
four new fabulous men to Harlequin American Romance.
Whether they're rebel ranchers, millionaire power brokers
or sexy single dads, they're all gallant princes—and
they're all ready to sweep you into lighthearted fantasies
and contemporary fairy tales where anything is possible
and where all your dreams come true!

You don't even have to make a wish...Harlequin American
Romance will grant your every desire!

Look for Harlequin American Romance wherever Harlequin
books are sold!

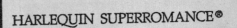